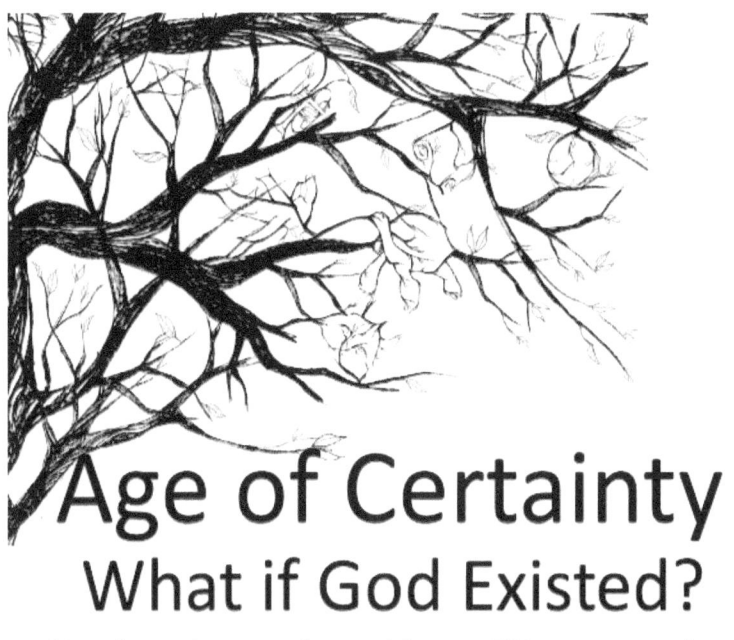

Age of Certainty
What if God Existed?

Edited and Introduced by William Freedman
Illustrated by Élena Nazzaro

James Morrow
Jeffrey Witthauer
Ian R. Thorpe
Patrick Evans
Brian K. Lowe

Jennifer Rachel Baumer
Brandon H. Bell
James Hartley
David J. Fielding
Ron S. Friedman

Rebel ePublishers
Detroit New York London Johannesburg

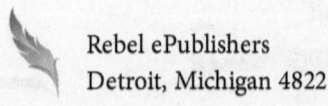

Rebel ePublishers
Detroit, Michigan 48223

ISBN-13: 978-0-6157807-3-3
ISBN-10: 0615780733

Cover design by Élena Nazzaro
Interior design by *Caryatid Design*

Copyright Acknowledgements

The Second Coming of Charles Darwin © 2013 by James Morrow
In the Company of Gods © 2013 by Jennifer Rachel Baumer
Atomic American and the Adventure of the Divine Question © 2013 by Jeffrey Witthauer
Manna © 2013 by Brandon H. Bell
A Divine Legacy © 2013 by Ian R. Thorpe
Accident Prone © 2013 by James Hartley
Mouth of Satan © 2013 by Patrick Evans
Time Stops for No Man © 2013 by David J. Fielding
Commitment © 2013 by Brian K. Lowe
"By the Way That He Came" © 2013 by Ron S. Friedman

TABLE OF CONTENTS

Introduction

When *Age of Certainty's* call for submissions went out, we asked for stories about how the world would be different if we knew for a fact that God exists, or that He doesn't. Considering how speculative fiction writers of my acquaintance are overwhelmingly atheist, I assumed they'd take this as an invitation to put paid to the whole concept of divinity. Other non-deists might have a character named "God" who mucks about, and we would draw from a smaller but more fervent cadre of authors who'd make their case in favor of the Lord of All. *Age of Certainty* was to be an evenhanded collection of stories postulating both the existence and non-existence of God.

That's not what happened.

The first thing that became apparent once the reading period opened is that genre writers – as much as they consider theology to be complete hokum – love their speculative elements, and the ones who submitted the best work all took the position that God is among us. Without making a blanket statement, my further correspondences with the selected authors suggests that they, as a general rule, have little to no religion in their lives – but that doesn't make God any less a fascinating character to them.

The next thing that I noticed is that there are quite a number of devout Christians who write speculative fiction. I was really rooting for one of them to break out of the slush pile with a story worthy of inclusion here. Sadly, all I got from that choir was Jesus Christ fanfic devoid of any social commentary, but replete with wish fulfillment.

I confess I'm disappointed by the paucity of good stories submitted which posited that it's unlikely that God exists. Certainly, nobody can prove a negative thesis, but you can prove that there's a simpler, more elegant explanation for phenomena up to and including the existence of the universe. Stanley Schmidt has no trouble filling up *Analog* with such tales every month, but *Age of Certainty* got few takers. Sadly, that handful of hard science fiction authors who did submit all misinterpreted the submission guidelines. They spent so much time on theory that they made the same mistake as the Bible thumpers and missed the whole point of the book: What would be the effect on society?

Still, I'm happy with how this collection ended up, whether through Divine intervention or happenstance. It's my privilege to present to you tales from ten talented authors who answer the question, "What if God existed?"

William Freedman
West Hempstead, N.Y.
11 February, 2013

The premise for this anthology is that there is proof, one way or the other, of God's existence or non-existence. Of course, any of us who have ever been falsely convicted of some minor offense know that there is proof and there is "proof." What if there were indeed "proof" of God's existence, but only because it was planted?

Here is a factual statement to preface this fiction collection: *Age of Certainty* was inspired by James Morrow's Godhead trilogy. Naturally, we asked him to write a blurb or, if he would be so kind, a foreword. Instead, he magnanimously offered us this gem of a story. To the best of our knowledge, this is the only tale ever told from the perspective of a talking, cybernetic tortoise which travels through time and shoots lasers out of his eyes. Only Jim could write something that could be thus prefaced without a "spoiler alert" disclaimer.

THE SECOND COMING OF CHARLES DARWIN

JAMES MORROW

If you saw me on the street, you would think I was just another giant Galápagos tortoise. The taxonomically inclined might even mutter, "*Geochelone elephantopus.*" Of course, if you in fact came upon a reptile of my size in an urban setting, your first reaction would not be, "That looks like a genuine specimen!" but rather "If the tortoises have escaped, can the alligators be far behind?"

Tortoise, *elephantopus*, fugitive from a zoo: appearances to the contrary, I am none of those things. Call me an automaton or, better still, a cyborg, for I can trace my tangled ancestry all the way back to that late-1970s educational initiative whereby school children would write rudimentary computer programs that sent iconic turtles scurrying across cathode-ray tubes. By the argument of John 1:1-14, in the beginning was the Word. From my pixelated perspective, in the beginning was LOGO.

Your Dr. Freud once remarked that anatomy is destiny, but for me anatomy is largely a nuisance. Although my legs are relatively long, I cannot scurry, LOGO-style, merely waddle briskly at two kilometers an hour. This velocity is sufficient for most of my needs. Send me word of a sunset, and I'll normally manage to reach the western side of the island in time to catch the chromatic crescendo. Occasionally I dream of sprinting, and once my subconscious mind reshaped me into a *Buteo galapagoensis*, a Galápagos hawk, soaring across a clear equatorial sky. On my more melancholy days I feel like an immense split-roll sandwich, my delicate self pressed between carapace and plastron – though at least my shell is of the saddle-backed variety, its raised edge allowing me to elevate my head like a periscope. How I pity my dome-backed cousins (I suppose I should say "metaphorical cousins," but the bond goes deeper than that) with their truncated necks and stubby limbs.

All cyborgs have a favorite joke. Here's mine. A well-known scientist, some say Bertrand Russell, once gave a public lecture on astronomy. He described how the Earth circles the sun and how the sun in turn orbits the core of our Milky Way galaxy. At the end of the lecture, a little old lady at the back of the room got up and said, "What you have told us is pure rubbish, sir. The world is really a flat plate resting on the back of a giant tortoise."

The scientist gave a superior smile before replying, "And what is the turtle standing on?"

"You're very clever, young man," the old lady said, "but you can't fool me. It's turtles all the way down."

Of the geniuses who cobbled me together I can tell you almost nothing. No names, no faces, no gossip. I am better informed concerning my programmer, Dr. Madirakshi Chatterjee, the closest entity I have to a mother or, for that matter, a father, an aunt, an uncle, a first cousin – a lineage. I was manifestly not made in Dr. Chatterjee's image, and yet, in a gesture I can only call loving, she supplied my inner speculum with a photograph of herself, so that I might periodically draw comfort from her soothing smile and beatific demeanor. By human standards she is a handsome specimen, with high cheekbones, dark luminous skin, and raven hair as thick and luxurious as the plant-matter rafts on which the seminal Galápagos species, drifting westward from South America on the Humboldt Current, first reached these black and ragged shores.

Galápagos, Spanish for *tortoises*, and the place I shall always call home, for it was on the Isle of San Cristóbal that my keeper, Mr. Paisley, activated my circuits, ushering me into consciousness amid the sweet music of a hundred indigenous finches warbling their approval of the dawn. Consulting my brain, my *think tank* as I call it, I learned that Mr. Paisley belonged to the Friends of Genesis, a religious organization at whose behest I had been assembled. Following its construction by the Syzygy Institute and its ensoulment by Dr. Chatterjee, my unconscious carcass was loaded into the cargo hold of an Airbus and flown from Los Angeles to Mexico City. A second jet whisked me to

Quito, Ecuador, where I was transferred to a helicopter and borne to San Cristóbal along with Mr. Paisley, Mr. Paisley's associate the Reverend Mr. Tappert, the physicist Dr. Karactacus, and – the *sine qua non* of our project – a Fontanel-7000 high-definition chronoclast.

Beyond these snippets of my prenatal history, I was also given to know that my human companions meant to employ the Fontanel-7000 in an audacious experiment involving my displacement from the present to the year 1835. According to my think tank, time travel was now, and had always been, a reckless technology, more art than science, and yet if all went well Mr. Paisley and I would soon be hurtled back two centuries, on a mission so momentous that its details could not be entrusted to even so stalwart a tortoise as myself. So there I stood, ten minutes old and counting, digging my claws into the sand of Stephen's Cove and tingling with anticipation over my forthcoming adventure.

Whistling in counterpoint to the omnipresent finches, Dr. Karactacus alternately paced the shore and puttered with his chronoclast. He was a squat and roly-poly man, not unlike the inquisitive penguin who'd just wandered onto the scene. Although its function was transportation, the Fontanel-7000 did not remotely resemble a vehicle, but instead took the form of a dozen meter-high cones. I descended into my think tank. *Data scan.* The cones were called "Dirac lattices." Once arrayed in a perfect circle, they would become a portal to the past.

As Dr. Karactacus set about deploying the Fontanel-7000, my keeper stripped off his street clothes. Mr. Paisley was an earnest young man covered in skin that was by turtle criteria distressingly smooth. No shell, no claws: he looked so terribly vulnerable. The next thing I knew, he'd swapped his three-piece linen suit for an ensemble comprising water-repellent trousers, boots, coat, and hat. *Data scan.* He had chosen to disguise himself as a 19th-century whaler, though my think tank could not tell me why.

"State your name," Mr. Paisley demanded, guiding me into the shadow of the helicopter.

Data scan. "Omar, sir."

"Omar, you are one lucky machine. Of all cyborgs presently on the planet, you alone are specifically programmed to do God's will."

Data scan. "God" was the construct through which humans accounted for themselves. God was their maker, their sustainer, the ground of their being. God was their Dr. Chatterjee. "I am pleased to be of use, sir." It was an automatic response – I'm an automaton, after all – and yet I agreed with myself. I was indeed pleased to be of use. Whatever my purpose, I aspired to fulfill it with distinction. I wanted to do Dr. Chatterjee proud.

"Omar, there's something we need to know," said the Reverend Mr. Tappert, sidling into the conversation. He was a pale and blobby creature, as vulnerable as Mr. Paisley, though his uncarapaced condition aroused no protective instincts in me. "Can you distinguish a good idea from a bad one?"

"Dr. Chatterjee gave me many positive qualities, among them" – *data scan* – "a moral compass and an ethical barometer."

"We need to put your conscience to the test," Mr. Paisley said.

"Of course, sir."

"Racial supremacy, the notion that some categories of humanity are intrinsically worthier than others – is that a good idea or a bad idea?"

"Bad," I answered without hesitation.

"Excellent," said the Reverend Mr. Tappert. "And child labor, the practice of putting preadolescents to work in coal mines and factories instead of giving them an education – good or bad?"

"Bad," I replied.

"Splendid," said Mr. Paisley. "Now let me pose the most important question yet. Imagine you have an opportunity to prevent the worst of all possible ideas from entering human affairs – what would you do?"

"Dr. Chatterjee would wish me to leap at the chance," I replied.

"Indeed," said the Reverend Mr. Tappert.

"Though I'm not much of a leaper," I added.

Before we could continue this fascinating discussion, Dr. Karactacus appeared and guided Mr. Paisley and me toward the chronoclast. No sooner did we reach the hub than Reverend Tappert joined us, embracing his colleague in a protracted gesture of farewell. Tears glistened in both men's eyes. They trembled as if adrift on an ice floe, though the ambient temperature hovered near twenty degrees Celsius.

"Greater love hath no man than this," said the Reverend Mr. Tappert, "that a man lay down his life for his friends."

Data scan. The New Testament. John 15:13. And suddenly I understood why their sorrow ran so deep. These two Friends of Genesis did not expect to see each other again. In truth the Fontanel-7000 was not a portal but a pit – an irredeemable descent into that slipperiest of abysses, the cavity of the elapsed.

Now the Reverend Mr. Tappert retreated to the perimeter, joining Dr. Karactacus and the penguin. The physicist pulled a remote control from his pocket and pressed a plastic button as round and red as – *data scan* – the eye-ring of a female Galápagos frigate bird. Instantly the Dirac lattices began to glow like rigging swathed in St. Elmo's fire, their overlapping auras spreading across the beach to enter the surf beyond, so that the Humboldt current became a Charybdis of white-hot metals roiling in a crucible. I cast an admiring glance on Mr. Paisley. Here was the face of heroism, I thought. Here was the countenance of courage. I would do anything to keep this man from harm. Greater love hath no cyborg than this, that a cyborg lay down his life for his keeper.

Into the flux, then. Into the chronofoam, the spacetime soup, the tachyon gazpacho. For an indeterminate interval we rode the shimmering vortex, wayfarer and tortoise, destination 1835. At first I knew only unremitting fear, as would any sentient creature caught in a metaphysical blizzard, but then I summoned Dr. Chatterjee's smile to my speculum, and I calmed down sufficiently to exchange a few sentences with Mr. Paisley.

"Are you available to yourself, Omar?" he asked. "Are you cognizant of the stuff within?"

"I know what I know, sir." The maelstrom disgorged a serrated fragment of infinity. I ducked inside my shell just in time to avoid decapitation. "But like Socrates I don't know what I don't know."

"Your visual system was not designed solely to receive data from the electromagnetic spectrum," Mr. Paisley reported. "It boasts a second purpose."

Data scan. The man had spoken truly. My ocular apparatus was dualistic. "Rather like the vertebrate penis," I noted. Mr. Paisley blushed. "Each of my eyes can emit a beam of coherent light. My brain likewise has two independent functions: cognitive operations and nanobot storage. The latter capacity is localized in my prefrontal lobes, which presently contain ten thousand discrete clusters of molecular machines. On receiving its orders from my CPU, a given cluster will follow the nerve pathways to my retinas and then proceed along the laser shaft like a band of pilgrims crossing a bridge."

"'Pilgrims' – good word choice."

"Doctor Chatterjee's word choice, actually, sir. She has a poetic nature." *Data scan.* "Each nanobot cluster is marked for a different destination. We shall variously target birds, reptiles, and mammals, though in every case the species will be one to which Mister Darwin paid particular attention during his trip to the Galápagos."

With scorn in his voice and a sneer on his face, my keeper asked, "What else do you know about this Darwin?"

The maelstrom spit forth a luminous portion of eternity, large and massive as a millstone, but luckily the thing bounced harmlessly off my shell and spiraled away. *Data scan.* "Charles Darwin, British naturalist, author of *On the Origin of Species by Means of Natural Selection, or the Preservation of Favored Races in the Struggle for Life.*"

"Such a learned turtle."

"According to Mister Darwin, the staggering biodiversity of our planet owes to a phenomenon he termed 'descent with modification.' Even its supporters admit that the theory is counterintuitive, yet when we factor in certain other aspects of physical reality – the vast tracts of time, the unimaginable amounts of death, the incalculable quantities of copulation, the appalling impermanence of ecological niches – we end up with a robust scientific explanation for why living creatures look and act the way they do, or so the Darwinists insist."

"Evolution – the single worst idea ever to spring from a human mind."

"I'm sure you're right, sir."

"Thanks to Darwinism, millions of children have come of age believing they are nothing but pieces of meat, and hence the nightmare of modernity – atheism, abortion, fornication, feminism, homosexuality."

A light went on in my silicon brain. "I see it, Mister Paisley! I see my mission! We're going back in time to assassinate Mister Darwin!"

"Nonsense, Omar. You should know me better than that."

Data scan. Assassination was not an acceptable Christian *modus operandi.* "You have a different strategy in mind."

"Throughout the five-year voyage of the *Beagle*," my keeper said, "Darwin subjected hundreds of vertebrates to scrutiny, collecting one biological oddity after another. Years later, pondering the fruits of his travels, he became intrigued by certain striking similarities between animal specimens drawn from allied but distinct species. Eventually he recalled that most of these different-but-similar creatures had been isolated from each other by some extreme geological circumstance: a lava flow, a mountain range, a large body of water. He then jumped to a conclusion that the separation had *preceded* the speciation."

"How impetuous," I said.

"Impetuous, impulsive, rash, and wrong. From this fatal error flowed Darwin's supposition that none of the species he'd observed on the voyage was a product of special divine creation. Rather, he had encountered only the descendants of descendants of descendants."

"Turtles all the way down."

"What?"

"An old joke."

"There's nothing funny about atheism."

Once again my cranium incandesced, only this time – I

11

knew it, knew it, absolutely knew it – this time my insight was genuine. "Eureka, sir! Eureka and eureka again! We're going to meld the species! We're going to nip Darwinism in the bud!"

Before my keeper could reply, a pullulating piece of forever broke loose from the maelstrom and came spiraling toward me. I attempted the usual turtle retreat, withdrawing inside myself, but before I could make the move everything went black – black – black as Galápagos lava – black as the smoke from Darwin's pyre – black.

I awoke to the growl of the surf grinding against the pinnacles of volcanic tuff ringing Stephen's Cove. Now a second polyphony reached my ears, the arias of the San Cristóbal finches. As my head cleared, other psalmodists joined the choir. A swallow-tail gull, according to my think tank, plus a dark-rumped petrel, a masked booby, and a vermilion flycatcher. High among the trees, a mockingbird performed a plagiarized cantata.

Peering out of my shell, I was surprised to find my field of vision filled not with blue equatorial sky but with brown San Cristóbal sand. In a matter of seconds I correctly interpreted the anomaly. I had become that most pathetic of creatures, a tortoise on its back.

For a full hour I suffered my supine circumstances, my head bobbing about on its leathery stalk, my legs rowing in all directions, until at last I heard Mr. Paisley's voice.

"My dear Omar, I was afraid we'd lost you in the vortex!" he cried.

"Give me a hand, will you, sir?"

Mr. Paisley set both palms against the edge of my shell and

rocked me back and forth, which accomplished nothing except to make me feel dizzy and nauseated. Next, he brought his shoulders to bear on the situation, but despite much puffing and groaning he failed to flip me. At length he thought to improvise a lever from a piece of driftwood, and thus it was that, thanks to my keeper's ingenuity and Archimedes's insight, I once again found my feet.

I glanced in all directions. The Fontanel-7000 was gone. The Reverend Mr. Tappert and Dr. Karactacus were nowhere to be seen. Strangely enough, a Galápagos penguin had come down to the beach, a distant ancestor, no doubt, of the curious bird who'd watched our departure in 2025.

During my involuntary dalliance in the soup, Mr. Paisley explained, he'd visited with Nicholas Lawson, the Galápagos vice-governor, appointed with Ecuador's blessing following that country's appropriation of the archipelago. Mr. Paisley had presented himself to Mr. Lawson as an American whaler who'd swum ashore after pirates scuttled his vessel. The vice-governor bought the story, and the two men had then passed a pleasant morning discussing their mutual devotion to the God construct. Before the encounter was over, Mr. Lawson offered Mr. Paisley bed and board at the gubernatorial mansion until such time as the castaway obtained transport back to his native New Bedford.

"May I assume that Mister Lawson also provided you with temporal orientation?" I asked.

My keeper cackled with delight. "Evidently Doctor Karactacus scored a bull's eye. Today is September the eleventh. Darwin won't arrive until the seventeenth. In short, God has granted us six days in which to accomplish our project. I suggest we start immediately."

"Ready, willing, and able, sir," I said, wishing Dr. Chatterjee had not provided me with quite so many bromides.

Mr. Paisley noted that if Darwin was planning to visit all fourteen islands, we might find ourselves in a time crunch. But if we assumed that the naturalist's second coming would be a recapitulation of the first – a logical necessity, Mr. Paisley believed – he would explore only four: San Cristóbal, Floreana, Isabela, and Santiago.

"Six days," I mused aloud. *Data scan.* "God made the world in six days, and we shall consume the same interval in making evolution extinct!"

"Well said, my dear turtle!"

Mr. Paisley led the way across a vast, shimmering slab of pahoehoe lava, scored and ropy like an immense black cerebrum. My think tank informed me that throughout the seventeenth century the Galápagos archipelago was known as *Las Encantadas*, the Bewitched Isles, so named because the ill winds and capricious currents would commonly collude to mire a ship in the doldrums, leaving its crew to die of thirst. Straggling across the bleak volcanic field, I could easily believe that some malignant magician had once counted this place among his favorite *pieds-à-terre*.

My sluggishness obviously irritated Mr. Paisley, but he was too polite to mention it. Instead of urging me to move faster, he editorialized on our sorry surroundings, lamenting the stunted trees, thorny cacti, prickly thickets, coarse lava, stark craters, and pocked cliffs. He particularly reviled the huddled clans of sea-going lizards, and I could not dispute his judgment, for these beasts were singularly hideous and exceptionally ill-natured.

14

"At long last I understand the Galápagos," Mr. Paisley declared. "Welcome to Eden West, Omar, that pathological Paradise, with iguanas instead of the Serpent. Make no mistake. It was on these very shores that mankind's Second Fall occurred, and I would hesitate to say which catastrophe was the worst, the primordial loss of grace or the subsequent lapse into Darwinism."

We began with the leaf-toed geckos. Carefully, cautiously, I fixed my gaze on the first such lizard we encountered, a yellow-bellied *Phyllodactylus tuberculosus*. My laser beams froze the target in place, and then the nanobots got to work, scuttling along the glowing viaducts, then swarming across the gecko like ants encountering an ice cream cone. With programmed virtuosity, the mites went to the heart of the matter, the gecko's genotypical essence, deftly transforming the animal into a green-bellied *Phyllodactylus genericus*.

I focused my beams on a second specimen, and – zap – *tuberculosus* became *genericus*. I transformed a third lizard, then a forth, a fifth, a sixth, dozens, scores, hundreds. A full morning's work, satisfying in ways I could not articulate.

"When we go to Floreana later in the week," Mr. Paisley explained, "we'll turn all the Baur's leaf-toed geckos, the *Phyllodactylus baurii*, into *genericus* as well. Later we'll visit Isabela and likewise refashion the Galápagos leaf-toed geckos, *Phyllodactylus galapagoensis*."

"My nanobots are at your command."

Tuberculosus, baurii, galapagoensis: three separate species, Mr. Paisley elaborated, three separate acts of divine creation. But Darwin in his perversity had refused to see that stone obvious truth. By 1837 he'd become a full-blown evolutionist, insisting that the Galápagos geckos all sprang from a common ancestor – a progenitor that had itself evolved. Thus it went, a path that took you as far from God as it was possible to go, back to the Permian, the Carboniferous, the Devonian, the Silurian, the Ordovician, the Cambrian, back to mud and nothing.

We spent the afternoon massaging the San Cristóbal mockingbirds, *Mimus melanotsis*, and by sundown we'd modified that "glorious instance of special creation," as my keeper put it, into an equally attractive *Mimus genericus*. Upon our arrival on Floreana, Mr. Paisley informed me, the nanobots would apply their talents to *Mimus trifasciatus*, leaving behind a thriving population identical to the new and improved San Cristóbal kind. Landing on Isabela, we would upgrade *Mimus parvulus* to an animal that would not give Darwin the slightest pause.

"The mockingbirds are particularly crucial," Mr. Paisley informed me. "Most people would tell you the finches. They're wrong. It's the mockingbirds."

Data scan. My keeper had his facts straight. Shortly after leaving the Galápagos, Darwin had found himself pondering the differences among the various sorts of *Mimus* he'd encountered. If *melanotsis*, *trifasciatus*, and *parvulus* each occupied its own separate island – which seemed to be the case, though Darwin couldn't be sure – this circumstance would "undermine the stability of species," for why would God bring forth distinct kinds of mockingbird in habitats whose climate and geography were essentially identical? Eighteen months later, during a visit with John Gould of the London Zoological Society, Darwin found his suspicions confirmed: *melanotsis*, *trifasciatus*, and *parvulus*, Gould revealed, were confined to San Cristóbal, Floreana, and Isabela respectively – as was *macdonaldi*, endemic to Española, which Darwin had not explored.

"But it *does* make sense for God to have wrought four different types of *Mimus*," I said, though just then the explanation eluded me.

"Of course it makes sense," Mr. Paisley said. "With God Almighty, all things make sense."

As previously arranged, my keeper spent the night at the vice-governor's mansion. I remained on the beach, basking in Dr. Chatterjee's smile. At one point a party of six tortoises waddled into my vicinity, obviously wondering who this stranger might be, but reptilian curiosity is a paltry commodity, and before long they were ignoring me again. Shortly before dawn a lone male of pansexual proclivities approached me with a libidinous proposition, but I turned my back on him, and he let the matter drop.

Mr. Paisley appeared shortly after 9 a.m. and we immediately started fixing the San Cristóbal rice rats, *Oryzomys galapagoensi,* several specimens of which Mr. Darwin had apparently captured and studied during his visit. I asked Mr. Paisley why we were bothering with this particular creature, there being no evidence that *Oryzomys galapagoensis* had ever influenced Mr. Darwin's thinking, and he pointed out that, in keeping with their program, the nanobots were turning the rodents not into *genericus* but rather into a continental variety, *xantheolus*, a species from which, many a twenty-first century evolutionist would aver, *galapagoensis* had descended.

"I don't know if Mr. Darwin saw a South American *xantheolus* during the voyage of the *Beagle*," Mr. Paisley said, "but why take chances?"

Next we turned our attentions to the lava lizards, wringing *Tropidurus genericus* from *Tropidurus bivattus* in anticipation of our upcoming visits to Floreana with its *Tropidurus grayii* and Isabela with its *Tropidurus albemarlensis*.

As evening came to the archipelago, Mr. Paisley announced that we would now "homogenize your own metaphorical cousins." The thought sent a chill through my frame, and yet I couldn't argue with my keeper's logic. At one time fifteen varieties of giant tortoise had thrived throughout the archipelago, and while they represented but a single species, *Geochelone elephantopus*, they had nevertheless figured crucially in Darwin's corruption. A few days before the *Beagle*'s departure, Nicholas Lawson had remarked to Darwin that he could always tell on which island any given tortoise had been hatched. At the time Darwin did not make much of the vice-governor's boast, but eventually he came to appreciate its significance.

"I never dreamed," he wrote, "that islands about fifty or sixty miles apart, and most of them in sight of each other, formed of precisely the same rocks, placed under a quite similar climate, rising to a nearly equal height, would have been differently tenanted."

The great transmutation took until 11 p.m. with two thousand and forty-three members of *Geochelone elephantopus* poured into the *Geochelone genericus* mold. I took no pleasure in the procedure. Truth to tell, I found it repulsive. It is one thing to unleash nanobots on a lizard or a mockingbird, and quite another to tamper with your own brethren.

At last the distasteful task was completed, and an exhausted Mr. Paisley staggered back to his bed in Mr. Lawson's mansion. Were I a biological creature instead of a sentient machine, I wouldn't have been able to sleep that night. My anxiety did not trace entirely to our recent manipulation of the tortoises. What rattled me even more was the cruelty visited on my kind over the years by God's favorite species.

Data scan. Beginning in the seventeenth century, a steady stream of plunderers – pirates, whalers, fur traders – had routinely visited the archipelago to harvest its giant tortoises. In the days before refrigeration, *Geochelone elephantopus* was a dietary blessing for sailors stuck on a voyage of several years.

Data scan. Before the slaughter finally ended, well over two hundred thousand tortoises had been hauled away from the Galápagos. The animal was wiped out on three islands, and several subspecies became totally extinct.

Data scan. A common practice was for sailors to stack several hundred live turtles in the holds of their ships, one on top of the other. Though given not one drop of water or morsel of food, the creatures would nevertheless remain alive for months, perhaps a year. Suffering turtles all the way down.

"Big day ahead!" Mr. Paisley said cheerily, striding across the lava field in his baggy whaler's outfit. "No time to lose!"

He led me to Stephen's Cove, where a coracle bobbed about in the surf, moored by a hempen line to a natural volcanic pylon. In a gesture that made me feel like a second-class species indeed, my keeper disconnected the line from the pylon and secured it around my neck. While he could probably reach our destination entirely under his own propulsion, he explained, it would be best if I were simultaneously towing him.

The waters around San Cristóbal rose and fell with a ferocity such as I'd not experienced since the chronoclast vortex, and we crossed the fifty-four choppy kilometers to Floreana only through the most strenuous effort, Mr. Paisley paddling like a madman, me swimming furiously. Somewhere near the mid-point of the passage, I experienced an impulse to turn my head, bite through the towline, and let the current carry Mr. Paisley away, but my moral compass forbade this action. Eventually I felt pumice under my feet, and I struggled onto the shore.

If my keeper had any intimation of my belligerent fantasies, he kept it to himself. Instead he simply thanked me for being "such a reliable old tugboat" and proceeded to squeeze the salt water from his coat sleeves and trouser cuffs.

It was now two o'clock in the afternoon. For our opening gambit we remedied the geckos, *Phyllodactylus bauri* to *Phyllodactylus genericus*. My heart wasn't in it. Next we camouflaged the lava lizards, *Tropidurus grayii* to *Tropidurus genericus*. The procedure left me cold. Shortly after 4 p.m. Mr. Paisley ordered me to update the four hundred specimens of *Geochelone negri* gathered on the southern slope of the central volcanic cone, whereupon I looked my keeper in the eye and announced that I was no longer in his employ.

"How's that again?" he said.

"I'm quitting, sir. I simply can't do this anymore."

"You're not making much sense, Omar."

"Sorry, sir."

"Conform them – *now*."

"Maybe Darwinism is the case, sir. Maybe it's a delusion. I don't know. I don't care. I'm only a tortoise. But here's the truth as I see it. It's high time you humans stopped regarding yourselves as the apples of God's eye. The biosphere was not made especially for your benefit, and the sooner you acknowledge that fact, the better for the rest of us."

Mr. Paisley tore off his wide-brimmed whaler's hat and shook it in my face like a matador antagonizing a bull. "See here, Omar! I absolutely *insist* that you conform these tortoises!"

"No!"

"Do it!"

"Never!"

"Traitor!"

"Numbskull!"

"Reptile!"

"Parasite!"

Strangely enough, our disagreement generated a great deal of local faunal interest. From all quarters of the island the creatures converged on the southern volcanic slope. Not only the recently transmuted geckos and lizards, but hundreds of other denizens as well: sleek marine iguanas and majestic green sea-turtles, slithering Floreana snakes and fluttering red bats, proud sea lions and playful fur seals – and birds too, oh, lordy, yes, the birds – petrels, pelicans, crakes, cormorants, terns, shearwaters, herons, gallinules, stilts, flamingoes, pintails, oystercatchers, flycatchers, all of them screeching and squawking and cawing and warbling.

Now the birds began to land, most of them settling on the slope, the rest roosting around Mr. Paisley in a series of concentric rings, so that he looked rather like a time traveler standing at the center of a Fontanel-7000. Embarrassed by all this attention, he restored the whaler's hat to his head and sat on a nearby lump of pumice. He shouted something in my direction, but the avian cacophony drowned him out.

It was then that a kind of miracle occurred. I can think of no other term. As more and more creatures arrived on the slope, both my keeper and I were privileged to glimpse what Darwin had wrought, not the theory of natural selection *per se* but the issue of its loom, that astonishing tapestry in all its dimensions, height and width and breadth and time. For a luminous instant the woven wonder hovered before us, riding the wind like a silken tesseract, enfolding every beast and bird that now drew breath and had once drawn breath and ever would draw breath, each thread begetting the next. Not in some airy realm bereft of actuality but right here on planet Earth, so that by following the filaments you could, if so inclined, join a macaque to a mollusk, a bear to barnacle, a hare to a tortoise, a priest to a paramecium.

A dense and vital silence came to the volcano. The birds stopped screeching. The iguanas grew expectant. The geckos and tortoises crowded eagerly around us, intuitively aware that this was not a typical afternoon on Floreana.

"Make me part of it," Mr. Paisley said, rising from his chunk of pumice.

"Do you mean that, sir?" I asked.

"Yes, Omar. I do. Make me part of it."

"As you wish."

He reseated himself on the boulder. "It's good to be connected," he noted.

"There is no better condition," I assured him.

Carefully I trained my laser gaze on Mr. Paisley. He shuddered and gasped and opened his heart to his incipient transmutation, and an instant later the nanobots were upon him, redeeming his genotype. Dr. Chatterjee must have foreseen that it would come to this, because the little machines knew exactly what to do, *Homo sapiens* to *Homos genericus*, but they didn't stop there, of course – no, they kept on refining him, until at last he became a great egret with a shining breast and a crown that glimmered in the late afternoon sun, like snow on a mountain peak.

For a full minute the egret stood perched on the pumice, preening himself with his long elegant beak, and then he released a joyous cry, spread his magnificent wings, and flew away.

22

It took me the rest of the evening to clean up the mess we'd made on Floreana, restoring *Phyllodactylus genericus* to *Phyllodactylus bauri* and *Tropidurus genericus* to *Tropidurus grayii*. The following morning I swam back to San Cristóbal, where I spent the next twenty-four hours setting things right on that world as well.

Four days later, shortly after 10 a.m., the *Beagle* sailed into Stephen's Cove. In the shank of the afternoon, the ship's naturalist launched a dinghy and rowed himself to shore.

I took an immediate liking to Charles Darwin, a young man of twenty-three years, vigorous, affable, with a bulbous nose and kindly eyes. The lava slabs held no enchantment for him, but he was fascinated by my size and bulk and antediluvian aspect. He patted my head affectionately, then asked me – rhetorically of course – if he might sit atop my shell, and the next thing I knew the two of us had become a sort of chimera, the fabulous Minoturtle of San Cristóbal. I bore him back down to the beach. Before my new friend and I parted company, I experienced a nearly overwhelming desire to tell him who I was. Somehow I managed to keep silent, realizing that such a revelation might work some mischief on the spacetime continuum.

Thirty-seven days later I was accorded one last view the great scientist, stroking toward the *Beagle* in his rowboat. Within the hour, Captain Fitzroy weighed anchor. From my think tank I retrieved a sad fact: in all the forty-seven years that remained to him, Mr. Darwin would never return to the Galápagos. As the *Beagle* glided free of Stephen's Cove, bound on its course across the South Pacific, I stood on a lava spit and wept, and soon afterward an unfathomable loneliness came over me, weighing upon my body and soul like an iron carapace. I was triply marooned, it seemed – in my cortex, in the past, in *Las Encantadas.*

But you must not feel pity for me, for I harbor within my think tank a golden datum. Prime among Dr. Chatterjee's personal goals is an intention to visit the Galápagos before she dies. In a mere one hundred years, she will be born, and forty years after that her career in biocybernetics will flower, and her thoughts will turn to the archipelago of her desires.

It's a beautiful day here on San Cristóbal. The sea lions roar. The finches sing. The black iguanas slither into the bay. I wander the harsh volcanic shore, wrapped in solitude and bathed in hope, waiting for my creator.

If you're looking for proof of God, maybe your first question should be, "Which one?" Jennifer Rachel Baumer imagines a new era of prophecy, in which people know their gods exist because their gods speak directly to them and, in this case, live down the street.

Her story is for all the animal lovers out there and, judging by Facebook, that's everyone.

In the Company of Gods

Jennifer Rachel Baumer

God sat knitting in a decrepit rocking chair someone had thrown out onto the street. Two p.m. on a July dog day in Reno and God sat bareheaded directly in the sun, knitting something very long out of a kind of aqua yarn.

Chrissy's footsteps faltered when she came around the corner and saw God there, knitting. The day was hellish hot, and the neighborhood smelled of burning motor oil and old cat boxes or something, plus Montello Court was the kind of neighborhood where guys sold crack in the front yard, and sometimes people shot each other, but it seemed like a bad idea to tell one of the Divine Entities where she ought to be sitting.

Plus if there was a god, and more and more since the Age of Miracles had begun, gods had started appearing all around the planet, theoretically this god was the Christian one, and if she existed, then Hell existed, which meant she had created it and should have enough sense not to sit rocking and knitting in the center of it.

Chrissy stood still, staring, her blond hair wisping annoyingly into the sweat on her face, her very white skin burning in the supernova sunlight. She was loathe to walk down the street with God sitting there. Last time she ignored common sense and went where the gods were instead of going the other way, they'd mistaken Chrissy for Cassie and made her their oracle as they tried to restart the Trojan War.

"You planning to come down this street any time soon, girly?" God called. God's hair was sparse and the color of Northern Nevada summer-white clouds. She was wearing a dress from JC Penney. Chrissy's grandmother had one just like it.

"Depends," Chrissy called back. She was still right at the corner. She could run. Probably. God was four houses down.

Right in front of Chrissy's duplex. Of course.

"On?" God called back. She flipped the blue-green knitted thing out and studied it. "More stars?" she muttered musingly and then, "What does it depend on? Your ice cream is melting, by the way."

The ice cream had melted two steps outside the grocery store, but the Honda had balked today so she was on foot. That was the least of it. The time before when she'd gone where the gods were she'd gotten engaged to Thor. No one in her family had been amused and her stepfather had taken such offense he'd said something and Odin winged him with a huge icicle spear.

"It depends on quests. Is there a price for coming down this street?"

The ice cream had reached saturation level and was escaping

26

its little round pint container. Pralines and cream seeped through the bottom of the paper bag she clutched and dripped down her leg.

"Girl, there is a price for everything," God said, rolling up most of the yarn and tucking her needles into the big aqua knitted thing. Within its depths, something like stars glittered. "But this quest you might even enjoy."

"Does it involve war? Or fortune telling? Or me getting engaged to anyone?"

God sighed. "There are more scenarios for you to guess at than stars in this galaxy. Are you going to try them all? Because if so, I'm going to require an umbrella."

The ice cream was drying into a sticky cast on Chrissy's leg. Inside the grocery bag, the heat of the day was wilting the vegetables. "Would you like to come inside?" Chrissy asked. There was no point in trying not to sound resigned. God would know better. "I have some iced tea in the refrigerator."

"Delighted!" God grinned.

"No," Chrissy said.

God sat at the battered table in Chrissy's dingy kitchen and sipped her iced tea. The kitchen had sported peeling mustard-gold patterned wallpaper when Chrissy moved in a year ago, and still did – she was determined not to stay in the duplex long enough to remodel and willing to deny all evidence that she hadn't moved out yet.

Chrissy's four cats ranged around God, sniffing her shoes, rubbing against her calves and, in the case of Siberia ,who was known to be quite forward, sitting on God's lap. The three lost dogs of the week pressed up against the screen door on the infinitesimally small backyard porch. A flightless pigeon and an apparently blind or amazingly stupid blackbird shared a cage over the television, and three turtles her sister's boy had suddenly decided he was terrified of, battled to smell worse than the fetid hedgehog her nephew had rejected in kindergarten. Her nephew was 11 now. Who knew hedgehogs lived so long?

God was unperturbed by the menagerie, as befitted a supposedly benevolent deity.

"No?" God questioned. She sounded mildly amused. She had taken a small compact out of her atrocious and enormous purse and was touching up her cloud-white hair.

"*No*," Chrissy said emphatically. "I'm going on vacation with my *sister*. We're going to New Orleans. I have always wanted to go to New Orleans and so has Cheryl."

"Cheryl wants to go anywhere far enough away from home to make the decision to divorce the rat bastard that's her husband," God said calmly.

Chrissy raised her eyebrows. "You think Raymond is a rat bastard too?"

"No. Cheryl does."

Chrissy shook her head. "Good. I'm going to New Orleans. With my sister. On vacation. For *any* reason Cheryl wants to go. *It's all planned.*"

God tilted her head and looked at Chrissy sideways. "It's not jury duty," she said. "You don't get to just say no."

"You can't say no to jury duty, either," Chrissy said, staring out the screen door into the duplex's trodden-grass back yard. Dirt showed through as if the grass suffered from pattern baldness. The dogs spent time on her screened back porch while Chrissy tried to find their owners during the hours she wasn't working at the law office.

"At least the courts understand if you already have airline

tickets," she concluded finally and turned back around, expecting God had gone because she'd been so quiet for so many minutes. But God still sat there, sipping now from a frosty margarita Chrissy hadn't provided.

"What are you afraid of?" God asked. "Change? Your sister deciding on the divorce without your input? Hard work?"

Chrissy sat back down at the table and rested her chin on her hands. Her pale blond hair managed to drift into her face despite the fact there was no wind anywhere.

If I say all of the above, will she go away and let me go to New Orleans? Chrissy wondered.

"No," God said, as if Chrissy had spoken. "Come on, get your keys. We'll take a drive out to Washoe Valley and I'll show you the place."

The drive from Chrissy's really crummy Reno neighborhood to Washoe Valley took 20 minutes and deposited them in another world. She left behind duplexes and trash-strewn fence lines, and Walmarts and laundromats, and the constant smashing womb and heartbeat throb of every male from 15 to 50 and his lowered cave-like pot-smelling ride.

The valley housed some surprisingly spendy houses tucked up in the tree line against the base of Slide Mountain, which occasionally let go with large amounts of mud in the uncertain Northern Nevada spring and snow melt runoff. Across U.S. Route 395 to the east, desert sage circled tiny communities of less-expensive homes perched on the shore of Washoe Lake, a very-shallow lake that sometimes dried completely in drought years, leaving a sandy pit behind.

Chrissy's beat-to-death Honda chugged anemically through

the expensive homes and horse properties to the far end of the houses on the west side. Just before the really expensive houses on Franktown Road, a corner lot with three acres sported a ranch style house, an amazingly huge barn and completely screened-in exercise area. Inside the chain link were a collection of cats on one side and a bunch of dogs on the other. Outside the fenced-in barn, coming toward them, was a tall dark-haired guy with glorious shoulders and a discouraging expression.

"What is all this?" Chrissy asked. She was already freeing herself of the Honda, pocketing the keys. She needed to get over there and meet all the new cats and dogs.

Which probably required getting past the tall guy.

"This is the quest," God said. She stood right beside Chrissy, who hadn't heard her get out of the car.

Chrissy blinked. God briefly was a white-haired old lady, a column of fire, an enormous horse and what looked to be a rock. Then she was again a grandmotherly type with Kleenex in her sweater sleeves and a sugary goodwill that belied not taking no for an answer.

"This is an animal rescue designated shelter," God said, looking at the screened-in barn.

Chrissy couldn't resist. "And that?"

"Is the grandson of the woman who started it and who has been keeping the animals safe and who will die tonight."

Chrissy's head whipped around. "You can save her!"

It was very definitely a demand. What a horrible thing for God to just set out there.

God made a sound of dismissal that sounded like a tea kettle hissing steam. "That's not my job. My job is to see that there's someone available to take her place."

The guy with the shoulders had stopped to wrestle with a

golden Lab. The Labrador seemed intent on keeping him from going through the gate that stood a good 50 feet away.

Chrissy spluttered. "So, what? I'm just supposed to present myself to this woman as her successor and when she says, 'Successor? I don't understand,' then go on to tell her she's going to die tonight and needs me?"

The rest of her statement – I won't do it – went unsaid when the tall guy got free of the gate and dog and came close enough to hail them.

"Can I help you?"

"We're here about the job," God said, and unfolded a torn out piece of newspaper.

Chrissy read it over her shoulder as the guy with the shoulders crossed the grounds between them.

"Energetic animal lover wanted to train to take over animal rescue facility. Room and board and salary. Facility is full shelter status. Must love animals."

"You could have told me," Chrissy muttered under her breath as the guy came close enough to hold out his hand.

"I'm Sean."

Chrissy kind of lost her breath.

"I have My ways," God said to Chrissy without bothering to explain that to Sean, and then, to Sean, "*Hello.*"

She's *flirting*, Chrissy thought, horrified, and then, Can't blame her. The guy – Sean – had a great smile, all white teeth, desert-chapped lips. A straggle of dark curls kept falling over one eye.

Chrissy snapped out of her reverie because he was shaking her hand – he had very nice hands, strong and well-used, long-fingered, calloused – she could get lost there, too, just like with the shoulders – and asking them, albeit with confusion, if they wanted to come inside and meet his grandmother.

No, Chrissy thought, because if she was meeting anyone else it would be a great pack of grey stripe cats she could see rubbing on the fence, needing attention, and then, no, again, because their visit spelled his grandmother's doom.

It's natural, God said in Chrissy's mind. Truly, she doesn't mind.

Chrissy shook her head. Get out of my head. No deal. I don't like this.

God laughed.

Sean's grandmother sat at the kitchen table in the afternoon sunlight, reading a murder mystery. Her scrubbed kitchen featured granite counter tops, tile floors, bright yellow curtains and a handful of cats sleeping on spotless braided rugs, an arthritic beagle, a fat bassett and a balding parrot.

"Grandmother, these ladies said they came about a job. I didn't know—"

Lavender eyes softened at Chrissy and God as Sean's grandmother took them both in, one after the other.

"I've been expecting you," she said, generally to both of them at first and by sentence's end, only to God. She kept her thumb marking the pages of the book. "Sean, can you make us some tea?"

"It's 90 outside, Gran," Sean said. "Don't you think—"

"Tea would be lovely," God said. "Let's let them talk."

The tea was not lovely. It was Earl Grey and not a good one, so heavy on the bergamot it smelled like Yardley's English Lavender soap, and Sean had over-steeped it. He and God left together for the barn, where Chrissy watched them go with longing. She wanted to be in the barn, with the animals, not in the house with Sean's grandmother, about to have the exact conversation she'd already said she didn't want to have.

Lily made it easy. "Sean's going to have a hard time with this," she said, and when Chrissy stared, eyes wide, nodded. "Yes, I know who you are, or at least I know Who She is." She still hadn't released the book. It sat on the kitchen table, her thumb still marking her place. "And you, I'm thinking, are going to take over the shelter."

Chrissy shook her head vehemently. Her blond hair flew. "I don't have a clue how to do something like that! I just like animals."

Lily smiled. "And I have a few you'll like. Your Friend mentioned you have a degree in business."

Before Chrissy could debate "Friend," she went on.

"Sean knows what has to be filed with what agencies and where the funds come from. The house is paid off—"

"The house," Chrissy said dully. She'd imagined driving back and forth, the Honda dropping pieces here and there along the way, Nevada's gas prices soaring.

"You have ice cream on your leg," Lily said suddenly. "Did you know?" And then, without missing a beat, "Ask Her if she'll let me finish my book first. I want to find out whodunit."

Chrissy stood. "I'm going to … *go*, now," she said. "Thank you for the tea. It was— "

"Awful," Lily said. "Don't tell Sean. He thinks he does it well."

Chrissy raised her brows. "I'll have to, won't I? If we're going to be working together?"

Lily smiled, her features folding into a myriad of wrinkles. "Sean has the details of the job. He can introduce you to the menagerie, too." She winked unexpectedly. "Run along, if you don't mind. I have a book to finish reading."

Chrissy staggered into the yard and stood blinking in the sunlight.

God smiled and held out a hand. "You've done well today," she said, leaving no room to question that she knew everything that had passed between Lily and Chrissy. "Get your keys, we can go, and—"

Chrissy balled her fists and rooted herself to the gravel in the yard between the house and the barn. The world here smelled of hot desert dirt and sage. The distant mountains were blue and brown, the last of the winter snow gone in June. From where she stood, Chrissy could hear the low sleepy buzz of crickets and the scuttling confusion of quail. It was a different world entirely than Montello Court back in Reno, with its stench of burned oil and rumbling blare of stereos.

The ground itself seemed to feed her courage. "*You*," she said through gritted teeth at the little old lady holding her bulky pocket book. The turquoise yarn was trying to escape from the top of it. Distant lights twinkled within the folds of knitting. God looked unperturbed but very slightly surprised.

"*You*," Chrissy grated. "*You* are going to let her finish her murder mystery before you—" Swallow. The world danced crazily. "Before you do *anything*."

God smiled, benevolent, pink scalp showing through sparse hair. Just for an instant a burning rock stood in her place, glowering back at Chrissy. And then there were trees, ancient and twisted, and then a whale. Then there as God again, in an ill-fitting house dress, poking her knitting back into the bag using the needles themselves. The knitting seemed to be fighting back.

"Of course she can finish her book," God said. "What do

you take me for? The Devil? Everyone should get to find out whodunit." She gave a triumphant poke to the knitting, which subsided, and looked up at Chrissy. "Shall we go?" She indicated Chrissy's battered Honda in case Chrissy misunderstood her.

"No," Chrissy said resolutely and turned on her heel, stalking across the hot earth and gravel, sending several startled cotton tails away and alarming a group of quail into a rout where they pretended to fly. "I'm going to meet the animals."

Lily died. Sean called Chrissy the morning after they'd met. Lily's will left the house in trust to the shelter and the shelter to Chrissy and Sean. With an ease that smacked of a higher power than even the probate courts, the house, the shelter and the animals transferred to Chrissy and Sean.

Chrissy called in sick to her execrable boss, an attorney who hated everyone and everything everywhere. He threatened to fire her. She threatened to quit. Their pleasantries exchanged, he threatened to see her the next day. She threatened to be there. And then she hung up and drove out to Washoe Valley.

Arriving at the shelter was like seeing old friends again. The gray-stripe contingent wound around her feet. Orange cats purred and greeted her. A litter of kittens fit neatly into her hands, tiny purring balls of fur. The bobcat she'd had the honor of meeting remembered her, padding over on giant paws so she could scratch his head. On the other side of the enclosures one of the German shepherds growled at her but was outvoted by the Jack Russell terriers terrorizing her knee caps and the Labradors baying with happiness and the giant Saint Bernard who leaned on her until Chrissy had to hang on to Sean for support.

Sean held on to Chrissy a little longer than he really needed to in order to keep her upright.

"I'm glad my mother found you," Sean said. His smile was subdued. He watched the distant mountains as if waiting for something he didn't expect would ever really come. "I'm glad she placed that ad in the newspaper," he said.

Chrissy frowned slightly and tested the waters. "If she did."

Sean blinked at her. "What do you mean?"

Chrissy searched his eyes and saw nothing there. Neither guile nor knowledge.

"Serendipity," she said lightly. "As if it were meant to be. So that there didn't even have to be an ad."

Sean took a long breath and appeared to settle for pretending to understand what she was talking about.

He showed her the ropes, how and when to feed, explained about vet visits and feedings and the spay/neuter program enforced for new residents.

Chrissy squirmed. The degree in business – the one her mother talked about at length as if she'd paid for Chrissy's full-ride scholarship education – would stand her in good stead while she figured out the whole shelter thing, even if she didn't usually live up to her full potential, like her father had said, before he stopped living up to any of his and disappeared.

It might not be so bad here, she thought, following Sean into the barn and hoping to pet the bobcat again.

And that's when the county Animal Control inspector showed up.

"We're in compliance," Sean said. His voice was tight with anger.

The inspector moved through the barn as if the air were gluey or gravity was having its way with him. He was round, with a matching round face sweating in the heat already gathering in the morning. He wore his tan Animal Control uniform like a potato sack with the potatoes still in it. He smelled as if he'd been rolling around with several of the animals, unlikely because none of them seemed to like him, which Chrissy took as a warning.

Her temper wanted to flare. The guy whose nameplate read TOWNSEND had come waving official documents as though they were search warrants and she and Sean drug dealers or pedophiles or some worse combination. When the inspector told her to back off, that he intended to tour the facility alone, Chrissy tore the docs from his hand and pointed to the place that not only gave her the right to accompany him but demanded an employee from animal control be accompanied by a shelter worker. Working for an attorney who hated everyone including Chrissy hadn't been a *complete* waste of time; she'd learned to read for loopholes as a matter of habit.

Inspector Townsend had taken it badly.

"That's a bobcat," he said when the approached Bob's area.

Chrissy shut her lips tight and managed not to say "*Very good.*" She glanced at Sean and let him explain the circumstances that brought the animal to them and why he couldn't be returned to the wild.

Townsend, standing with his back to the chain link Bob paced behind, looked smug, like a bully who figured he had the upper hand. "I do not believe the license for this shelter gives you the legal right to house a dangerous wild animal here."

Chrissy, who had been tickling the Dangerous Wild Animal's belly 20 minutes earlier, coughed. It was cough or explode.

It was Sean who said, "We have the correct paperwork in place to legally care for abandoned animals including feral cats and dogs and wild animals surrendered by idiot humans who didn't realize what they were getting themselves into."

"I don't believe we need the commentary, Mr. Wells," Townsend said.

"I don't believe it matters," Sean said and Chrissy internally high-fived him, then thought about wrapping her arms around him and giving him a congratulatory kiss and made herself stop and pay attention to what was going on.

She looked at Townsend.

And saw a burning black pillar of flame.

She saw tornados and riots and haters hating. She saw legislation designed to stifle and kill. She saw animals being led to slaughter.

She yanked her vision back to the current reality and saw Townsend expounding his points to Sean Wells, whose anger trembled inside him, about to crest.

She saw Townsend continue his diatribe to Sean while his face slid sideways, malevolent gaze locking on her, the sharp-toothed smiles and the light in the black eyes that sucked her in.

"Christine Foley," the mouth said. "I know you."

"I know you, too," Chrissy said aloud because she had to break the spell, and as Sean's voice began to rise she stepped close to him and touched his corded tanned forearm, ran her fingers down his wrist and slid her hand into his, squeezing tight.

Sean shuddered and took a huge breath. "Everything is in order," he said.

The air around them sparked with rainbow lights.

"Everything is in order," Townsend said. His voice was confused. "*For now.*" As if he fought to free himself of heavy blankets.

"What do you mean we're not going to New Orleans?" Cheryl's voice was just short of a wail. "It's all *planned.* OMG, Chrissy, I need a break so bad, and I though you could – I mean, I wanted to – well, we'd have time, you wouldn't always be at the horrible job or making your car work or—"

Chrissy sat in her dilapidated living room, dangling her toes off the couch at the cats, who lay in the July sunlight, unwilling to move but clearly too hot to play. They stared at her sleepily with wise golden eyes that somehow reminded her of God's pacific blue ones.

What was it God had said over a pitcher of margaritas that had materialized from nowhere? "You're afraid your sister will make a decision for herself without your input"?

Very funny, God, Chrissy thought. As if.

Into the phone she said, "Cheryl, you know I'm always here for you," and overriding the automatic Cheryl protest that came in response, "I'll always make time to listen and to help. But we all have stuff in our lives. I have a living room full of boxes because I'm moving. I'd be happy to listen if you'd like to come help me move."

From somewhere she thought she heard God laugh again.

Surprisingly, Cheryl said yes. "I just have to pack up the kitten."

Chrissy felt a sinking. "Why? What's Justin done now?" Outside on the street a pair of brothers who looked like rejects from America's Most Wanted – *if you see them, don't call the police, the police are afraid of these guys* – were making a transaction with a middle-aged woman with gaps in her teeth.

"Nothing." The sound of Cheryl defending. "He just said kitty is too rough and she hurts him and he thought—"

Chrissy sighed. "Bring the kitten with you. And bring Justin, too."

An idea was forming somewhere.

"Oh, Chrissy, he'd never want to—"

"Cheryl Louise. You son is 11 years old. He's too old to be afraid of a kitten and you're his mother. Bring him. What else are you going to do, leave him home alone?"

"That's why I was thinking I couldn't come," Cheryl said.

"Bring them. Come. I want you to see everything."

Sean wasn't there when they arrived. His own house was 10 miles away in Carson City and the note on the whiteboard said he'd be back by evening.

"See?" Justin demanded. He wore Vans and skateboarder shorts and a T-shirt that either sported a very bleached out Bob Marley or a very bleached out Jesus, neither one looked thrilled to be on Justin's pre-teen chest. "Not even that guy wants to help you move."

Be careful, or I'll wave an eight-week-old kitten at you, Chrissy thought uncharitably. "Hey, _no_!"

But Justin, grinning, had already wiped the board of the rest of the message.

"Damn it," Chrissy said, and to Cheryl, who looked about to say, "Language," and get herself punched, "Did you see what the rest of that said?"

Cheryl shrugged, looking around the house. "Something about an inspector or something. Do we get a tour?"

They got a tour, Justin being chummily included because Chrissy didn't trust him to stay anywhere on his own. She carried the kitten with her, a warm purring bundle of fur and hope.

They ended back at the room where the kitten sat on a box of books Chrissy would need to unpack.

"She looks sad," Justin said, with more accusation in his voice than sympathy, but Chrissy tried anyway.

"Of course she does, sweetie. She's in a strange place and she misses you." Because she has no taste, but that's beside the point.

But looking at Justin for the first time, Chrissy saw uncertainty rather than fear on his face and thought of the first rat bastard who had left Cheryl all those years ago when Justin was six and impressionable and small for his age and facing bullies in his very first year of "real school."

Is that what it is? She thought, and then, *and that would be why Cheryl can't combat it.*

And she ignored the tiny tickle in the back of her mind that said Couldn't be the same reason you're consistently relationship-free, could it? In a voice that sounded suspiciously like God's.

You know, the voice went on. The whole abandoned by daddy thing?

"Shut up," Chrissy said, and Cheryl turned her head toward her but hadn't heard enough to ask.

"Hey," Justin said looking past the kitten and out the window. "Is that where the animals are?"

The barn was shadowy and warm, the late July afternoon filling the inside of it with the drifting ghosts of hay and dust motes.

"This is cool," Justin said. His flyaway corn-silk hair was the same color as the hay that piled in the corners. The barn, had been converted to a shelter, heatable in winter, cooled by breezes and shade in summer, with cat packs and dog kennels.

Justin's eyes lit he started to run before they were halfway to the shelter. Chrissy thought about calling, Slow down, you don't want to scare them, but the animals were waiting and she hadn't seen honest excitement in her nephew's eyes for a long time.

After Sean returned and whisked Justin away, Chrissy and Cheryl sat in a spill of sunlight just inside the cat run, leaning against the barn structure while Justin went for a tour, crossing back and forth from cats to dogs, always another resident he wanted to meet. The sisters sat with their backs to the barn and the southwest sun falling in their eyes and Cheryl made believe her tears were sun-caused and Chrissy let her for a while. When the shrill rusty sound of a magpie brought them both back to awareness, Cheryl said, "I'm going to divorce Doug." She didn't stop looking out at the foothills ringing them and the mountains farther on.

After a glance at her, Chrissy went back to staring at the mountains herself. "Good." Because she didn't know how to say she was grateful Cheryl had made the decision on her own. Or how she thought even being left by another father figure would be better for Justin than Doug was. Before she had to say anything, Sean appeared around the barn and said, "OK if I introduce Justin to Bob?"

Chrissy grinned. Cheryl, looking startled, glanced at Chrissy and asked, "Is it safe?"

"Very," Sean answered for her. "Some idiot was raising him as a kitten and when Bob suddenly turned into a bobcat, realized that was too hard."

Cheryl stuck her hands in the pockets of her jean shorts. "People are idiots," she said, sounding like the old opinionated pre-Doug Cheryl.

Chrissy suppressed a smile and followed them in, the four of them watching Bob as he jumped from loft to floor inside the barn, making the most of the not inconsiderable space he'd been given and coming back to have his ears scratched between athletic feats. Justin's face was a mask of wonder and delight: the all freckled, traditional, American boy. He was also the one who froze and said, "Who's that?" when the inspector entered the barn.

The bobcat didn't hesitate. The minute Townsend stepped through the chain-link gate and into the barn the cat sprang. Enormous spotted paws took the inspector's chest and shoulders and drove him down to the straw covered floor.

Cheryl screamed. Justin moved fast, scruffing the cat like it was any other house cat instead of a 35-pound wild animal. Chrissy moved toward the cat and inspector, hands out, mind going blank. Sean reached for the trank gun that hung off the wall out of cat reach but always there for humans.

Townsend never stopped snarling. Under the sounds of Cheryl and Justin and Sean shouting orders at everyone to get back and Townsend, still on the floor with his hands up, there was Townsend's ongoing tirade. About the animals and Lily, about light and life and things Chrissy didn't expect to hear in tones of fury and loathing. Her shoulders slammed into Sean's as she pushed past him, around Justin, and the cat Justin barely held off the man. Cheryl reached for her and Chrissy distractedly touched her arm. She needed to see Townsend's face.

Except he didn't have one. Townsend's face had disappeared into a moving mass of fury. Where features should have been, there were sharp edged teeth snapping, black eyes and far too many of them. Flames and fangs, knives and razor blades and sharp angry things that burned.

Beside her Sean leveled the trank gun to take the cat down.

Chrissy took it from him, her movements serene in the

midst of shouting, and snarling the cat growling, Justin suddenly crying out as the cat lunged free of him.

Chrissy fired. The dart struck Townsend in the shoulder. He jerked his head to look up at her and then screamed, part laughter, part fury, part something completely inhuman.

Townsend shattered into a mass of black spiders that poured from the place the dart had taken him. The spiders swarmed, gleaming black carapaces glinting in the hazy dust-laden air of the shelter.

Cheryl screamed, clawed at the walls and at Chrissy. Sean shouted and began to stamp his feet. Chrissy's mouth worked but not her brain yet. It was her nephew who said, "Be still," and turned when the spiders stopped moving and looked at her.

"Go back where you came from," Chrissy breathed at the spiders. "This is *my* place. This is *my* realm. These animals are under *my* protection."

Fire leaped up. Sean swore and stumbled backward, taking Chrissy with him by one arm and Cheryl by the other but by the time they'd backed away from the flames where Townsend had laid, the fire was gone. There was just the four of them, and Bob, who licked one front paw as though he thought he was an oversized house cat and crossed back over to Chrissy's side to nudge her hand, rub his whiskers along her thigh and wait for the stupid human to come to her senses and pet him.

And Chrissy, who didn't know anything about running a shelter but just loved animals, crouched and petted the bobcat.

God came to visit as summer slowed toward fall, a progression marked less by any reduction in heat or change in foliage, than by the noise generated by crickets. She brought Chrissy a turquoise afghan that unfolded out of her heavy black leather tote, and unfolded and unfolded, catching on the hard rounded tote handles and unspooling. Within the depths of it, stars twinkled.

Chrissy kissed her on the cheek. She'd become quite forward with deities; might as well since they kept behaving in very forward ways with her.

"You told me it was a quest," she complained once she'd finished rhapsodizing – and being a little afraid of – the afghan. It lay in a place of honor already, across the back of her favorite armchair. Her cats and Justin's kitten lay on top of the afghan. God seemed pleased.

"It is a quest," God said and sipped the tea Sean had made them. "This," she added, "is horrible."

Chrissy nodded. "Lapsang souchong. He's experimenting with smoked teas."

"In My Name, why? And why are you allowing it?" God wore a brightly striped caftan that made her look like a little old lady's head poking out of the top of a circus tent.

"About the quest," Chrissy persisted. "Quests begin and end. They start at Point A and go to a logical finite point, like B. Then they *stop*."

"Yes, they do," God agreed cheerfully enough that Chrissy looked over to see what she was drinking. Whatever it was, it was large, fruit-studded, sported a flower on top and smelled like rum.

"Can I have one of those?"

"Drink your tea," God said, smiling. "So. Your quest. It had a Point A and a Point B. What's the problem?"

The problem is flippant deities, Chrissy thought but far enough down to not be heard. "I also have a Point C, Point D,

Points E through H, a sister who is getting a divorce, which is good, but who keeps telling me about every step, which is not. I have a nephew who just discovered he loves animals and isn't afraid of them and who I think does magic and who is underfoot all the time. Did I mention the bobcat? And the guy who is actually a column of black flame or a bunch of black spiders, and who is trying to prove we are not in compliance here?"

God clapped her hands and laughed and drank more rum. "Very good! You're doing very well."

Chrissy took a breath. How was she supposed to tell God that God was missing the point? "The point is," Chrissy said. "It's not *ending*."

"Fabulous!" God said. "I knew you'd choose to walk down the street eventually. Now, about what I brought you."

Oh, I don't want to know about this, Chrissy thought. Being involved with gods almost never ended well.

God gestured at the easy chair where the cats were sleeping on the afghan she'd knitted. Lights still twinkled in its depths. To Chrissy it looked ominous.

"About the galaxy the cats are sleeping on," God started.

Voltaire wrote, "If God didn't exist, it would be necessary to invent Him. Let the wise proclaim Him, and kings fear Him." Well, if He did exist, might it be necessary to deny Him? Should intellectuals refute Him, and heroes oppose Him?

Jeffrey Witthauer takes us to a comic-book world in which war is a simple struggle of Good against Evil and primary colors obscure any shades of gray, wherein to pose these questions.

Atomic American and The Adventure of the Divine Question

Jeffrey Witthauer

Michael Mason shouted, "Give my regards to the Fuehrer, Ratzi!" as his rocket boots propelled him into the Nazi robot. With a swing of his mighty fist, the hero known to the world as Atomic American connected the lightning gauntlet – his latest invention – with the mechanical fascist's head. Electricity crackled at the contact point, and the head exploded in a shower of sparks. Michael threw up his arm to protect his face, and the sparks fizzled out harmlessly against his fireproof red-white-and-blue leather jacket.

"Mike!" cried Estevo, his trusty partner. "Help!"

Michael touched a button on the side of his mask, and auto-binoculars slid into place over his eyes as he scanned the

French countryside. He spied his brightly costumed companion fending off automatons by swinging his staff in wide arcs. The staff was made of a lightweight composite, strong enough to send the metal servants of the Third Reich scattering with each strike. But it would not be enough. A full twenty robots were approaching the Portuguese freedom fighter, and even his skill with his native martial art of Jogo do Pau would not save Estevo. At least, not alone.

"Time to test one of these babies," Michael said to himself, pulling a cryo-grenade from his utility belt. As he touched another button on his mask, the auto-binoculars were replaced by his new targeting system. He had designed the system with Alan Turing during the Adventure of the Stone Shark, then miniaturized it through Atlantean super-science to fit in his red domino mask, and what an adventure that had been!

But this was not the time for reminiscence. The Nazi robots were closing fast. Michael's targeting system measured the parallax between his right eye and his left to determine the distance of whatever he looked at. He watched as the Nazis approached and, when the proper range had been reached, he drew back his arm and threw the grenade toward them, showing off the arm of a former All-American quarterback. The grenade exploded in a flash of blue light, which faded to reveal the remaining robots encased in solid ice.

"Santa Maria," Estevo breathed.

"She had nothing to do with it," Michael said confidently. "It was a little something Doctor Hoenikker and I worked up last time we were in the States. Right after the Adventure of the Congo Gorilla, remember?"

"Yes, Mike, I remember," Estevo said with a nod. A fallen robot stirred and Estevo slammed the end of his staff through its cranium. "Where did the Nazis get robots?"

"No doubt from their secret alliance with the Reptilians of Thule, whose technology is powered by dark sorcery. I'm sure President Roosevelt will send the Stars and Stripes Squadron to look into it. Maybe I'll even volunteer to go along."

Whatever else Michael might have said was cut off by a high-pitched whistle.

"Mike! Bomb!" Estevo shouted.

Michael wrapped one arm around Estevo, leapt into the air, and once again activated his rocket boots. They were propelled along at fantastic speed, tousling Michael's short black hair, but only for a few moments before the bomb exploded and sent Estevo and Michael careening away. Michael landed on his back with a grunt and, as he looked skyward, he saw a huge, oblong shape shimmer into existence in the sky above. Then another. Then more.

"Nazi zeppelins!" he shouted.

"How did they sneak up on us?" Estevo asked as he jumped up to his feet.

"No doubt they were cloaked by Thule sorcery. Look! They're launching fighters!"

Each massive zeppelin was fitted with low-slung fighter bays which slowly opened, pouring forth the latest German rocket planes and jetpack soldiers. The sky became dark with the massive Nazi swarm.

"Jesu Christo, Mike, it looks like they sent the whole Luftwaffe after us!"

"Good! The more of them focused on hunting us the fewer of them to harass our fighting men on the front lines! I think it's time for a tactical retreat."

Michael and Estevo turned and began running across the war-torn battlefield. Michael attempted to activate his rocket boots, but the boots sputtered and died.

"Blast! Out of fuel!" he warned.

"We're not going to make it!" Estevo shouted.

"Yes we are! Just keep running!" Michael commanded. Estevo started praying under his breath. Michael did not.

Nazi rockets peppered the ground around them with clusters of explosions. Michael could feel the heat singe the hair on the back of his neck but he kept running. Luckily, Nazi super-science had concentrated on destructive force rather than accuracy.

"There! A trench!" He pointed to a rift in the ground, and the two heroes sprinted toward it.

Suddenly two rocketmen dropped down and hovered before them, aiming shoulder-mounted machine guns. Estevo reacted with a fighter's reflexes, throwing his staff toward the first. It struck him full in the face, causing him to career wildly and spray bullets at his companion.

"Nein!" the surprised target shouted as the bullets pierced his volatile jetpack, incinerating both of them in the ensuing explosion.

Estevo flipped upward and grabbed his staff as it fell, but even as he did so another chorus of whistles split the air.

"More bombs!" he shouted.

"I hear them!" Michael replied. They were almost at the trench. Just a few more yards.

The two men skidded into the trench just as the bombs struck. A tunnel led into the earth, and they rolled into it just before the entrance collapsed in a rain of dirt and rubble. For a moment the two men waited in the darkness, listening. They could hear the planes flying overhead, but no further bombs were dropped. Michael touched a button on his utility belt, activating his auto-light to illuminate the darkness. Estevo did the same.

Michael looked around at the concrete walls, stripped of equipment.

"Well. A standard Nazi bunker," he remarked.

"Nazi?" Estevo asked.

"Probably. The Nazis rarely fight from trenches, but they dig underground bunkers near the front to house and maintain their super-science forces. This one is abandoned now, of course. The front has moved, and so have the bunkers. Those Ratzis probably don't even remember it's here. It puts us in a bit of a spot, though. They can't get in, not through solid concrete buried under the earth. But we can't get out."

He tapped his mask to activate his miniaturized radio.

"This is Atomic American, repeat, Atomic American, special operative." Over an open radio he used the moniker by which he was known in the press. Michael was less concerned with maintaining a secret identity than some heroes, but a little caution was always warranted when Nazis could be listening in. "I hope you can hear me, boys, because we've got every Ratzi pilot in France breathing down our necks right now. We're going to hole up as long as we can, but we ..." he sighed, and turned off his radio. "It's no good. We're too far underground to get a signal out."

"So what do we do?" Estevo asked.

Michael smiled tightly. "I have a plan. But it's going to take a while. I need to do some calculations."

"We don't have any paper," Estevo pointed out.

"That's all right, I'll improvise." Michael took a marker from his utility belt, and began writing on the wall of the bunker. He moved slowly, aware that his every calculation had to be exact. What he wrote was a complex collection of mathematical symbols, combined with strange, arcane sigils.

"Mike?" Estevo asked.

Michael paused. "Yes, Estevo?"

"They call you Atomic American because of your genius. They say you're the smartest man in the world."

Michael laughed, modestly. "Well, I'm not sure you can measure that. And almost every one of my inventions was created with the help of the world's greatest scientists. Like this marker, which Laszlo Biro and I developed for—"

"The point is, you're brilliant," Estevo interrupted. "But you're an atheist."

Michael sighed at the turn in the conversation. "Yes, Estevo. I am an atheist."

He studiously turned back to his equations. Estevo, however, did not give up.

"Do you remember our first adventure together? The Adventure of Lost Aztlan?"

Michael smiled. "I do remember that."

Estevo planted his staff into the depression in the ancient temple floor, which opened the gate that blocked the serpent pit. Unfortunately, it also activated the dart guns and filled the air with poison darts. Moving like lightning the Portuguese hero pushed off with his staff, flying over the pit of serpents to the other side.

"Look out!" Michael shouted. His new companion had shown such bravery throughout this adventure, despite the strange circumstances and the improvised nature of his involvement. But now Michael could see that one of the ancient Aztec darts was hurtling toward the Portuguese Olympian. A single prick from the deadly Chupacabra venom it carried would kill him instantly. Without any options, Michael threw the only thing he had available: The sacred talisman of Quetzalcoatl. With perfect aim the talisman hit the dart, deflecting it. Estevo landed on the other side of the serpent pit, and the talisman shattered into a thousand pieces.

"The talisman!" Estevo cried. "But without it, how can we appease Tezcatlipoca?"

"We'll have to come up with something," Michael insisted, already deep in thought.

His thoughts were not given much time. From the center of the room rose a swirl of darkness and smoke, and there formed a mighty black jaguar with glowing green eyes, twenty times the size of the two heroes put together.

"Who has dared disturbed the sleep of Tezcatlipoca, god of darkness and shadow?"

Michael slowly tracked his gaze upward to the beast's sinister eyes, then stepped forward. "I am known as Atomic American. I represent the United States government."

"I know nothing of these United States. What gift have you brought to appease me?"

Estevo gave Michael a worried look. Michael did not bat an eye. "We had a great gift for you, Tezcatlipoca, but alas your protections were too mighty, and it was destroyed."

"So you stand before me now with no appeasement?" the mighty jaguar roared. "How dare you! I shall flay you slowly for a thousand years, then I shall terrorize the upper world as I bring forth the Age of the Jaguar!"

"Yes," Michael said quickly, "You could do that, but then you would not receive our greater gift!"

The jaguar god cocked his head. "What greater gift?"

"The gift of warriors and servants that I shall give to you!" Michael lied.

"These I can find easily on my own! For humans shall worship a god who walks among them. I shall now destroy you!"

"No, wait!" Michael called out. "That … that would be a mistake. Because while you have slept, another god has risen, who means to challenge you."

Estevo gaped, wide-eyed, at Michael's bluff. The jaguar god lowered itself toward Michael, its great green eyes narrowing. "What god is this, who would dare challenge Tezcatlipoca?"

"The great god, uh …" Michael said, and looked at Estevo, who looked back.

"Lincoln!" Estevo blurted.

"Yes, the great god Lincoln!" Michael echoed enthusiastically.

"And who is Lincoln that I should fear him?" Tezcatlipoca rumbled.

"Oh, he is a powerful man, and beyond that …" Michael faltered.

Estevo picked up where he had left off. "He is leader of a great Union."

"That's right, a union of gods! Washington, whose mighty axe fells whole forests, and Franklin, who calls down lightning from heaven, and Jefferson, who's, oh … very clever with policy." Michael hoped the ancient god would not see through him.

"And these would challenge me?" the jaguar god eyed them suspiciously.

Michael nodded. "Lincoln and his fellows are honored and, um … worshiped throughout our great United States. If you were to emerge without followers of your own, his armies might destroy you while you were still weak. But instead, we will give you the gift of followers. You need only give us time."

Tezcatlipoca drew himself up tall, and nodded. "Very well. You will have one thousand years to prepare my army to destroy this … Lincoln." The jaguar god dissipated into shadow and smoke, his booming voice delivering one last lingering warning. "But when that time is passed, I shall awake again."

Michael grinned. "We'll be ready, don't you worry."

"You met a god, Michael," Estevo pointed out. "How can you be an atheist when you've met a god?"

Michael smiled. "He's not much of a god if I can outwit him, is he?"

Estevo shrugged. "Well what about the Adventure of the Iceland Volcano? Do you remember?"

Michael nodded. "Yes, I remember."

Michael kept a firm grip on the Holy Sword of Saint Christopher and slashed at the demon, slicing through the foul beast, which disintegrated in a puff of sulfur. He kicked a second in the face, then threw the sword high to skewer a third as it flew down from above on leathery wings.

"Unhand Estevo, Beelzebub!" he demanded as he caught the falling sword.

"Mike!" Estevo shouted as he struggled against the demon lord's cursed manacles. "It's about time!"

The hideous Beelzebub rubbed his twisted and gnarled hands together, his scabrous body bubbling with pustules that burst into swarms of flies and crawling maggots. "You! But I had you captured and delivered to Lucifer! How did you escape the clutches of the Prince of Darkness?"

"Maybe Lucifer is not the ally you thought him to be," Michael said confidently. "Now set Estevo free, or we shall see how the Sword of Saint Christopher dispatches a demon lord!"

"Never!" the Lord of Flies buzzed. "He is the Seventh Seal, the last sacrifice that I need before the gates of Hell are thrown open, and my army of demons takes over the Earth!"

"Mike, for the love of Santa Maria, help me!" Estevo shouted as he pulled at his chains.

Michael pointed the Sword of Saint Christopher at Beelzebub. "Sorry, ugly. But the gates of Hell are closed for the day."

"Do your worst, mortal! Greater men than you have tried! Men with the true power of God on their side, and not just a blessed sword!"

Michael held the sword overhand, and threw it point-first. Beelzebub ducked and drew up one arm. At his gesture, the swarm of flies that constantly buzzed about him knitted together to form an impenetrable shield of darkness. The sword, however, never touched the shield, and instead soared over the demon's head.

"Ha! You have wasted your opportunity, mortal!" Beelzebub cackled. "You missed!"

"I wasn't aiming at you," Michael retorted.

Estevo whirled around, and pulled the sword, which had just cut through his bonds, out of the sulfurous stone behind him.

"Hey, demon," Estevo spat. "Go to Hell."

With one smooth motion, he drove the sword through Beelzebub's unprotected back.

The demon lord screamed as the tip of the holy weapon pierced through his belly. He dragged himself off the blade, and cursed, "Know this, mortals! I have marked you! You have not heard the last of Beelzebub!" His body slowly disintegrated into sulfur and dead flies.

"You've gone through Hell," Estevo protested. "Not figuratively. Literally. You slew demons with a holy blade from a dead saint."

"Well yes, I can see how that might imply God," Michael equivocated. "But it's not a sure thing."

Estevo stared at him, wide-eyed and incredulous. "Beelzebub mentioned God by name!"

"Look, it never hurts to be skeptical, all right?"

Estevo sighed wearily. "All right, leaving Hell aside, for the last few years you've worked with the Stars and Stripes Squadron."

"Yes, fighting the Nazis on special missions from President Roosevelt."

"And that didn't convince you that there is a God?"

"Should it have?"

"Remember your teammate Samael? Remember the Adventure of the Zombie Reich?"

"My lightning rod is having no effect!" Michael shouted as he drove the crackling staff into another zombie, the electrical discharge firing uselessly into dead flesh. "Baron von Skull's creations run off magic, not electricity!"

"Then perhaps I can help," spoke Samael, his voice ringing through the entire room like it always did. He gave a great flap with his mighty wings, then soared over the zombies, his body shining with a heavenly aura. "In the name of the Silver City, and all the Hosts of Heaven, in the name of the Alpha and Omega whom I serve, in the name of God Almighty, I declare this ground to be … holy!"

Samael drew his great flaming sword, and with both hands

plunged it into the ground. A blast of light emanated forth, sweeping outward in waves. As it washed over each zombie the creature jerked, and then fell lifeless to the floor. Baron von Skull desperately worked the controls of his Necromachine, to no avail.

"*Nein, nein, nein*! How could zis happen! Vat haf you Amerikaanerz done!"

"Your castle is now holy ground, von Skull," Samael proclaimed in his holy voice, which filled the room like the booming thunder of a divine hurricane. "No evil creature will arise here. You have a chance now to turn from your sin, and embrace the Lord's light."

"*Nein*! I shall defeat you, angel!"

Von Skull raised his gun and fired. The bullet halted half an inch from Samael's flesh. Michael ran up and knocked von Skull out with a punch to the jaw.

Michael shook his head. "I still can't believe Baron von Skull tried to shoot an angel with a Luger. Samael's been a public hero since the thirties. Everyone knows you need satanic weapons to hurt him."

"But that's my point!" Estevo protested. "You worked side by side with an angel of God. Samael has had personal, intimate conversations with the Lord Almighty. How can you still be an atheist when you have gone out for drinks with an angel?"

"To be fair, Samael didn't actually drink," Michael joked. "He just went with us for the conversation."

"Mike!" Estevo said, exasperated. "He wrote a book about being an angel, describing heaven and God in detail. It was a best seller. You own a copy. Thanks to his witness, and the witness of others like him, the number of non-believers in the world is statistically insignificant."

Michael sighed. "To claim that God exists is perhaps the greatest, most extraordinary claim one could make. I cannot just take Samael's word for it, even if he is an obviously super-human being."

Estevo frowned. "Fine," he said begrudgingly. "What about the Final Adventure?"

"What?"

"The Final Adventure."

Michael rubbed his temples. "It was not the Final Adventure. It was the Adventure of the Rosicrucian Vault."

"The papers all called it the Final Adventure."

"It was not the Final Adventure. I have had adventures since then. We are currently on an adventure that has come after the so-called Final Adventure."

"Still, it was almost your Final Adventure, wasn't it Mike?"

Michael remembered.

"There's no way to stop it," Estevo gasped. "Da Vinci's entropy generator will overload, and cause the heat-death of the entire universe."

"There's always a way to stop it," Michael insisted. He looked at the sparking panel, crackling with alternating bands of blue and black energy. "There. If I manually connect those contacts, the power will be shunted into the ground before it can build to critical levels."

"You can't do that!" Estevo insisted. "Coming into direct contact with chaos energy will kill you!"

Michael looked at his partner, sadly. "Estevo … it's the only way."

Estevo knew. Michael could see in his eyes that Estevo knew. "Goodbye, my dearest friend."

"Goodbye, Estevo. The world still needs heroes. Be what the world needs …."

Michael touched the contacts, and his world faded to white.

When Michael awoke, he was atop a shining, silvery balcony, looking over a city so grand, so magnificent, that he knew in a million years he would never be able to properly describe it. A Silver City, just as Samael had told him so many times. He checked himself to see if he was dreaming, or hallucinating. All his senses seemed to be functioning perfectly. All the signs told him what he was experiencing was real. He heard the beat of wings, and Samael himself landed before him.

"Samael! What are you doing here?"

"I wanted to invite you into the Silver City myself, my friend." He gestured behind him. "Welcome to the afterlife."

"But I was never a believer in your God. Shouldn't I be, you know … in that other afterlife?"

"All will be explained to you. Come with me."

Samael led him along jeweled streets, and through gates of pearl, and along rivers of gold. Michael was overwhelmed with feelings of peace, and joy, and love for the entire universe. Finally they reached a tower that stretched up and up into infinity.

"The next step on the path is your own, Michael. I cannot enter."

Michael looked at the tower with trepidation. "Is … is He in there?"

"See for yourself."

The gates of the tower swung open, and Michael walked inside. Sitting at a table, sipping coffee, was a man in a robe that glowed white like the stars, eclipsed by His long, white beard.

"You don't mind if I look like this, do you?" God said. "I do so like living up to expectations."

Michael flushed. "That's not Your real image, is it?"

"All images are My real image, Michael. I am everything and anything I desire to be. Now. Let's talk about you."

"Yes. Not that I'm complaining, but shouldn't I be in Hell?"

God smiled. "Do you think you deserve Hell?"

"No. I've led a good life. I've tried to help people and make the world a better place."

"There you go then. I'd say you've been a pretty good follower of Mine."

Michael frowned. "I've never followed You."

"Michael, I created this universe for the creatures that live in it. Anyone who helps those creatures follows Me. You've been to Hell. Did you see any tormented souls?"

"No," Michael admitted. "Only demons."

"There you go. Some people think they need Hell, and so Hell is there for them. But between you and Me, I wish they'd get over it and come here." God smiled.

"So, what am I going to do for eternity?"

"Well, that's the question, isn't it?" God stood up, and turned away from Michael, clasping His hands behind His back. "You're a hero, Michael. It's in your blood. I think you would be pretty bored without adventure."

"That's true," Michael agreed.

"But things are just about perfect here. There's no crime for you to fight, no evil dictators for you to defeat. Most other heroes, well, they would consider this to be a well-deserved rest. But you've never been one for resting, have you, Michael?"

"No, I haven't."

God nodded. "I thought not. Well, I suppose I had better send you back then."

"What?"

"I said I suppose I had better send you back. You'll be miserable here with no people to save, and we can't have miserable people in Heaven. It defeats the whole purpose. You want to go back, right?"

"Yes," Michael said with finality. "Until all evil is eradicated from the Earth, I want to keep fighting."

"There's a question you want to ask Me first though, isn't there Michael? A question about your wife?"

Michael hesitated. "No," he said quietly. "I have to be honest, I don't actually want to know the answer to that question."

"Interesting," God mused. "Well, back you go."

Michael felt a tug in his soul, and soon he was falling through clouds, with the earth below him.

Michael sighed, writing down more figures on the wall of the bunker.

"You met God," Estevo said. "Not a messenger from God, or a representative from God, or a fleeting dream or image of God. You went to the Silver City, you talked to God, and then you were resurrected by God. And don't pretend that you think it was a hallucination or something like that. Samael later confirmed your entire story."

Michael frowned, but said nothing. He just kept writing his equation.

"I have traveled with you for years now, Mike. I have seen you save the world more times than I can count. We were adventurers together, then heroes, then soldiers against Hitler.

And I've never brought this up before, because I never thought it was polite. But now I have to know: How can you call yourself an atheist?"

"Because it's easier than explaining the truth," Michael murmured.

Estevo frowned. "I beg your pardon?"

"It's easier than explaining the truth." Michael turned, and looked at his companion. "Of course I'm not an atheist. The servants of God Almighty, and scores of lesser gods and demigods, interact with this world directly and tangibly on a regular basis. I'm not an idiot, and I'm not blind. I am a rational man, and in a world with angels and demons and more, all rational men have to admit there is absolute, incontrovertible proof of God. So obviously I'm not an atheist."

"So what are you then?"

"An anti-theist," Michael said. Then he shook his head. "No, even that's too simple. I'm not against God. I just don't trust Him."

"But, Mike," Estevo explained patiently, "He's God."

"We're fighting perhaps the most evil man the world has ever known. Adolph Hitler is a mass murderer. He's a monster. So why does God allow him to exist? Why does God not reach down and fix whatever madness makes him evil? Why did God not keep him from rising to power?"

Estevo shrugged. "I don't know, but we know God exists, and we know God is good, so He must have a plan."

"Except we don't know He's good. We know He exists, but we don't know He's good. And that's my problem. There is such evil in the world. Such pointless, destructive evil."

Michael reached up and wiped his suddenly stinging eyes. "I used to believe, you know? There was so much evidence for God, of course I believed. I went to church every week with my wife. My beautiful wife. And then she died." He laughed bitterly.

Estevo paused, then said quietly, "But she's in a better place now. You've seen it."

"How? How can a place apart from the person you love be better? I would choose her over Heaven in a moment, and I know she felt the same way." Michael closed his eyes, his voice faltering. Even after so many years he still felt pain. "That was the start. I thought, how could a loving God take my wife away? And through a drunk driver, no less. So very pointless."

"You became a hero because of that tragedy," Estevo insisted. "You went down to Mexico to clear your head, and that is where you met me, and we had our first adventure. You have saved the world, time and time again, and all that good came out of the tragedy of your wife's death."

Michael closed his eyes. "That's what I tell people. Again, it's easier than the truth. But didn't you ever wonder why I was already prepared to be a hero that first time? That first adventure was supposedly so spontaneous. Haven't you ever wondered why I already had my utility belt, my gadgets, even my mask?"

"I ... I just thought you were a man who was always prepared."

"I was prepared to be a hero." Michael turned back to his formula. He did not pick up his marker, he just stared at it. "I was prepared to be a hero, because God was not a hero. Because God let people die. God let madmen rise to power. Because under God's rule, the world has seen a history of barbarism, murder, superstition, and fear. Now maybe that's because God isn't as powerful as people believe. Maybe God needs heroes to pick up the slack. But I've always thought it was something different."

Estevo's eyes had widened in shock, but he had heard too much to stop his friend. "What have you thought?" he prompted.

Michael looked over his shoulder, and his soulful eyes met those of his partner. "We have all the evidence we need that God exists. But we have very little evidence as to His character. How do we know God's on our side? How do we know God is good? He's a superhuman being that, from what we can tell, rules the universe. But does He rule it as a benevolent guardian? No. He demands worship. He demands churches. He demands obedience."

"Does He really?" Estevo asked. "He was going to let you into heaven, and you don't give Him any of that."

"He seemed to think I do, despite myself. He said I had been a good follower. And has Samael, or God Himself, ever said that the church which insists He deserves worship is wrong? Maybe it is men, not God, that insist on worship. But God seems to lap it up all the same. In my mind, that makes him no more than a dictator, like Emperor Hirohito, or old Adolph himself."

"Mike, you can't say that about God!" Estevo insisted.

"Why not? I could say that about Roosevelt. I could say President Roosevelt is an evil dictator. I'd be wrong, and people would tell me I was wrong, and people might get angry because they love the President, but they wouldn't call it blasphemy. But you can't do that with God. And that makes me suspicious. Anyone who demands to be worshiped makes me suspicious. It speaks of ego, and evil. Anyone who claims to be our Shepherd, but allows evil societies to flourish, makes me suspicious. It makes me think He's really on the side of the bad guys, or playing some larger game with us as pawns."

Estevo shook his head. "I think that sounds pretty paranoid."

"Maybe," Michael said. "Maybe. But even after we've taken down every earthly dictator and tyrant, there will be one grand Tyrant that remains. And I intend to prepare for that. Better to be prepared than sorry." He sighed. "So that's why I call myself an atheist. Because it's a lot simpler to let people think you're a fool who does not recognize the evidence, than to explain that you see the evidence all too well, and it frightens you."

There was nothing Estevo could say to that. He looked at his friend now with concern. Michael hoped there was some revelation mixed in with the concern. Finally, Michael picked up the marker and drew the last few equations. "There, it's done. We can get out of here now."

"What is it?" Estevo asked.

"A summoning spell. I was given it a while ago, and just had to figure out how to triangulate our current position."

"You don't normally use magic," Estevo said in surprise.

"I do when I have to. Here we go."

He began chanting in a strange, heavy language, one filled with thick, screeching consonants that seemed to scrape against the soul itself, and as he did so, the marks on the wall began to glow with black fire. Estevo stepped back and gripped his staff, ready for anything. Suddenly the bunker filled with a burning bright light, which coalesced into the shape of a man sculpted to physical perfection, with a sensual face and athletic proportions, his beauty marred only by the large red bat wings sprouting from his shoulders.

"You wish to conclude our bargain?" Lucifer asked Michael.

"I do. We need exfiltration from this bunker. If you could make us a hole out of here, and scatter the Nazi forces outside, I'll consider us square."

"Very well. With this, my debt to you is concluded."

Lucifer held out his hands, and hellfire flowed from them, blasting a hole in the wall. He flew out with a great beat of his wings, and the air filled with the sounds of Nazi machinery exploding.

"You made a deal with Lucifer?" Estevo accused in shock.

"More like he made a deal with me. Remember when Beelzebub had you captured?"

"How could I forget?"

"Well I didn't find you at first. Hell is a pretty big place. I was captured and brought before Lucifer."

"And you made a deal with him to escape?"

"No, I escaped on my own. I made a deal that I would embarrass Beelzebub, who was a contender to the throne of Hell. In return, Lucifer would do me an unspecified favor in the future. So I rescued you, and you ran Beelzebub through with a holy sword, which embarrassed Beelzebub in front of the entire satanic host. By the time he reconstituted himself he was a laughing stock, in no position to challenge the throne. So Lucifer owed me one."

Estevo could say nothing. He just stared at Michael.

"Like I said, it's one thing to know these beings exist. It's another entirely to know their motivations. Now let's go pound some Ratzis."

According to at least one neurobiologist, there is a protein that predisposes people toward religious yearning. Criticism came quickly from both scientists and theologians. In his 2004 general readership tome *The God Gene: How Faith is Hardwired Into Our Genes,* Dr. Dean Hamer answers his detractors from both sides by stating, "This book is about whether God genes exist, not about whether there is a God."

Brandon H. Bell draws upon an interplanetary cast of characters to explain the distinction.

MANNA

BRANDON H. BELL

"You're gonna crash it," Chase said. He guided his plane in lazy circuits that grazed low over the hilltops.

My mouth opened to tell him to shut up when I heard my plane sputter and go silent. I looked up and saw it falling toward the slope below us.

"What happened?" I asked.

Chase watched with a raised eyebrow and a grin of smug disdain. I'd heard it so many times before: We-should-do-this-on-Saturdays. I didn't like his attitude after church. He wanted to save me. Or lead me to the Lord. However it worked.

He brought his plane down to a gentle landing at our feet and his chin into a satisfied nod.

I held my tongue as we hobbled down the slope to the crash. There were other pairs and small groups flying RC planes, kites, or picnicking. Most were fathers and sons or younger men and women. A few looked our way with sympathetic expressions.

I wondered, when we stepped to the side of the wreckage, if we were the first in the world to see it.

The plane had not stalled or failed: it had been hit. The loaf of bread, bulging with seeds and hot as though just removed from an oven, rested a foot from the crashed model.

"Bread?" I asked. I looked at Chase. He turned pale and stared at the loaf. I smelled it. Warm yeast and flour, coriander seeds and roasted sesame. It smelled delicious. I gazed, transfixed.

A yeasty, savory sleet broke the spell.

We turned to see, not hail, but more loaves of bread.

"Manna from Heaven," Chase whispered.

Weeks passed before the ships were spotted, and it rained manna every day like clockwork. An amateur astronomer noticed the torchships as they passed inside Neptune's orbit and then other, more powerful telescopes trained on the small fleet. Twenty-three craft in all, riding the torches backward as they course-corrected for Earth. Experts estimated a three-year maneuver, then reduced their estimates to six months when the ships flipped and completed the arc inward under acceleration. A final reverse burn came at the end just before they slid into orbit. I drove out to a family friend's house in the country who'd taken on the old Dobsonian telescope dad and I built in better days. I wanted to see the ships myself.

Almost everyone ate the manna.

I didn't.

On the hill, all those fathers and sons and pretty couples ate until stuffed and then laid in the grass and went to sleep. Chase did the same.

"Chase, what are you doing?" I said, shaking him.

"Tired man. All is good. No worries," and with that he went to sleep. I couldn't wake him. Then I thought of Dad.

I ran.

Down from the hill, cursing Chase for his stupidity.

When I reached the old man's house, he was sprawled in the back yard next to a pile of branches. The aroma of the bread wafted in the air and his hand clenched a half-eaten loaf.

"Dad?" I yelled. I cried as I lifted his stick-like limbs and heaved him in lurching steps across the lawn and into the house. I poured him into the Lazy Boy and propped up his legs.

Then I checked his pulse.

I sat staring at him until he woke an hour later.

"What the hell, Dad?"

"Danny. It's a miracle," he said.

"Come on, Dad, you're not that soft-headed," I said.

"No, Danny. You don't understand," he said, gesturing at the television. "Look. Look."

But there was nothing on the television.

Nothing that I could see.

God spoke to everyone. Over the radio. On computer and cell phone screens. On television. God was on iTunes and His voice even echoed from the grooves of records. All media reverberated with the Grace of His voice.

So I was told.

America fell to the Church years earlier. The *Message*, embedded in our DNA, emboldened the politically motivated on the right to declare governance their responsibility.

The *Artifact*, an inscribed sphere found in Africa at coordinates predicted by the *Message*, languished in the Smithsonian beside a monument of the Ten Commandments.

Clarkists, Crickists, and Dickian groups proposed alternate interpretations of the *Message*, but were minority voices most people regarded as kooks, atheists, or worse.

Then the manna rained, and with it God arrived.

Some people in the media didn't eat the manna. They did not last long in the New World.

We stopped hearing from comedians suggesting it might not be such a good idea to eat something that fell on the ground from who-knows-where.

"And did I mention that a fleet of alien ships is going to be here soon?" one late night host mentioned.

I snickered but Chase gave me a raised eyebrow and the next night a curt nod when the show aired with a new host.

"Bless us all, our living God," the slick-coiffed refuge from TBN intoned.

"What is happening?" I asked, without expectation of an answer.

"Look, man ... a new rain will fall today. Just try some. You don't have to have faith. You can see for yourself," Chase said.

"Doesn't that, I don't know, contradict the whole point of faith?" I asked.

"My Lord, Danny, why so difficult all the time? Why not just be a bit open?" Chase replied.

I laughed.

"I don't buy into anything that I have to take a pill in order to 'get'. It's not reality."

"A pill? You don't have to take a pill."

"No, I have to eat the bread falling from the sky. What's the diff? And that comic was right: there is a fleet of alien ships coming. Doesn't that strike you as odd?"

Chase smiled his trademark smile. Back in high school it was this certainty that made him cool in my eyes. Always ready to pronounce on the other guy's folly.

"It makes perfect sense. God had to act. These aliens are coming and because of the *Message* and the *Artifact*, God had to appear so the aliens can't side with the Clarkists and act like our long-lost daddies."

"Maybe I'll become a Dickian. They're the only ones that seem vaguely sane anymore." I countered. The Dickian's took the old science fiction writer's *Exegesis* as their bible. We'd talked about it before and Chase had dismissed the position with a quip about 'people who'd watched *The Matrix* one too many times.

"Solipsism," Chase said now, without explanation. He left and I sat in my apartment brooding.

The *Message* is in our DNA. It is a sequence of definitely artificial origin. Scientists tell us as much but until the coordinates in the *Message* were used to locate the *Artifact,* I did not believe. After they found the silver sphere engraved with the same numerical sequence there could be no doubt. Humanity and all life on earth had been created.

The Intelligent Designers filled school boards, rewrote text books. So-called Clarkists and Crickists battled with them. Into these circumstances rained the Manna, appeared God, and soon would arrive the aliens.

The day before the aliens were due to reach orbit Chase came to me one last time, excited.

"Danny. It's time for us to go home. You've got to eat the bread that God supplies us this day," he said, holding my hands in his. I yanked away and went to the TV. I meant to ignore him but static filled all the stations. The world was high on God. Nothing else mattered. I turned and saw him gazing adoringly at the screen.

"Jesus Christ," I said, turning off the set.

"Danny. The rain comes in a few moments. This is your last chance. We're going home, brother," he walked toward the door and stood there awhile, hand on the knob.

"Look, Danny, I know you've never really believed. Look at this as a break. No more blind faith. Just eat the bread and you'll see for yourself. Please, Danny. I don't want to leave you behind," his head turned away from me, tears falling from his face.

"What the hell, man? This is insane. Look, let's say you're right about this God stuff. A just God would respect the – how would you say it? – the intellectual honesty of me sticking to my guns. I really don't believe, see? I'm not rebelling by not believing in God, any more than I'm rebelling against Santa Claus. But something is wrong here. Can't you see that?"

"I'm sorry, Danny," Chase said. He wiped his face. "I love you." And with that his hand twisted the knob and he walked out the door. I never saw him again.

I sat on my leather sofa in my stylishly furnished bachelor's spread while my stomach tumbled in beat to the pulse at my temple.

The rain of bread came not long after and I turned on the stereo and scanned through the channels to see if any broadcasts remained. Just one.

"Today's rain of Grace has fallen. Praise be to the One God, our Heavenly Father. Brothers and sisters, go out and feast on the Grace He has bestowed upon us. Please, I beseech you.

"Today is the day of Rapture. Today, my fellow children of the Lord, we go home. It's only minutes now."

I turned off the stereo as the phone rang.

"Hello."

"Danny. I'm gonna see your momma today, Danny," the old man cried. Sobbed. I could barely understand his words. "Danny, are you gonna be there with us? Danny, you know your momma will be heartbroken if you're not there. Danny. Please, Danny. Please, son. I know I was hard on you all those years ago. Please just this once, son. Just this once trust your old Pop. Go out and eat your daily bread, son."

"Dad," I said, as only a son can say to his father.

We changed in that small gap of silence. Settled into ourselves, one last time, in relation to each other.

"The Rapture is in fifteen minutes, Danny," he said, as a matter of fact. "I hope to see you today in Paradise," and with that he hung up the phone.

He did not answer when I called back.

Fifteen minutes. It took twenty to get to Dad's house. I grabbed my keys from the counter and ran out the door, down the stairs, and into my tattered SUV.

I drove fast. From the apartment in Benbrook to the old man's house in West Worth was a rural drive along the outskirts of town. On the winding, two-lane road I glanced out to the arable fields, golden with loaves of bread. Cars and trucks lay strewn along the road like the husks of abandoned deities while huddles of people in the fields raised their hands to the sky. Even with the windows closed the smell of coriander, sesame, and yeast stifled. Drifts of bread-dust wafted across the tarmac and whirled in the Isuzu's wake.

My belly roiled. Bread falling from the sky for weeks, aliens sliding into orbit, and a God as silent as ever. What if I'm wrong ... about everything? Just pull over. The two people who love you best say so. Go eat the damn stuff. The thought seemed reasonable, and the same internal dialog that made me less decisive than Chase.

I shook my head.

Sweat beaded on my forehead. The SUV rolled among cars parked on both sides of the road. People thronged the field. Their hands raised as they showed their smiles to the sky. The sight freaked me out just as displays of fervent belief always did.

I looked back at the road, brakes screeching as I twitched to avoid a pink VW left in the median. I cursed and slowed to a careful twenty miles an hour, wiping the sweat from my brow with the back of my hand.

I glanced at the field. The empty field.

I slowed the vehicle.

The field: full of sunshine and trampled grass and loaves of bread and vortices of dust. But the people, all gone.

"Raptured," I said out loud. "Okay."

The stomach again. I'd need antacids soon or I'd not sleep tonight. I drove to the old man's house but knew what I'd find. Or, rather, what I'd not find.

Walking around the house, I discovered little of value to me. A few pictures from when mom lived. The baseball and mitt she bought me for my tenth birthday. A rosary the old man brought back from Europe.

"I love you guys," I said to the empty house, and left.

I went on a pilfering spree the next day. New clothes, new car, some guns.

I got a shotgun, decent rifle and scope, and a Glock that felt sleek and deadly in my hand. Ammo to go with. I loaded a Range Rover with various provisions, stocked up on bottled water and dry goods. There was a great water filtration unit at the outdoors store. No one questioned my activities. The stores stood deserted.

I thought about where to go. I could live anywhere. Hitch a trailer to the Rover and hightail it to Colorado, Toronto, Seattle. Wherever.

But with everyone gone, I stayed close to home. My imagination made it too frightening to venture far. At least right away. I kept expecting the giant locusts or whatever Revelation talks about to come down through the roof to eat my entrails like spaghetti noodles while I watched. Sounds stupid, but that's the kind of thing I drove myself to nightmare about those first few nights. Sweating like a pig at 2:00 a.m.

Fear has a way of making you numb, given time. I just wanted the wrath of God, or the demons, or whatever, to get it over with. Come on, already. I stood in the middle of the ballpark in Arlington and screamed it to the sky the following Saturday.

Broadcasts stopped. There *were* other people. Everyone ran and hid when I saw them.

I saw a kid on one of my trips to the mall and chased him through several stores, yelling that I didn't want to hurt him. It bothered me to imagine what it must be like for the kid, alone. But he was too scared to let me near.

I yelled that I'd be back the next day if he wanted to talk and the next day the mall loomed deserted. I sat on a food court bench all afternoon. The kid needed someone to take care of him, but he was too scared to let me help.

The mirror of his situation to my own troubled me. The kid had good reason to be scared. Crazy people in the world. Did God, if there were a God, look on me the same way?

Thing is, where I yelled about being back the next day, God apparently didn't give second chances. The rain of bread stopped the day of the Rapture. What was left behind had turned to dust by the time my doubt led me to look.

Despair filled my world like the faith of all those Raptured believers.

An evening spent with the Glock, pondering the frailty of human existence, came to an end when the weakness twisted into something new. And I knew what to do.

I found a telescope, equipment to make a relatively high-powered laser (not, like, alien-blasting powerful but line-of-sight-on-a-clear-night-from-surface-to-orbit powerful) and a switch that would let me do Morse code with it. I thought of dad, who'd taught me these arcana once upon a time: building telescopes, using Morse code, performing triangulations on a maneuvering board as he once did in his Navy days. Before he'd lost his wonder and replaced it with faith. I added a GPS unit and the latest iPad to my bounty.

That night I set up the telescope on our hill, the hill where Chase and I flew the model planes, and trained it on the torchships stationed in the sky. Not geosynchronous, I concluded, but in an orbit that took them across the entire globe. Made sense.

I set the telescope to track one of the ships first then programmed in the relative location of all twenty-two of the other vessels. Then, with the laser mounted to the telescope, I spent the next few nights typing in my Morse code message in twenty-three five-minute bursts.

On the fourth night I gasped when I looked up toward the faint tracers of the ships and saw twenty-three strobing lights, signaling back. Morse, even.

"Rendezvous at coordinates 13:00 hrs GMT -6:00 tomorrow," the twenty-three lights flashed. Over and again until they slid out over the flank of the planet.

When the aliens arrived, I stood unimpressed. Life and limb didn't matter. I wanted to know why they did it. I guessed it was obvious: they needed the planet and the God routine, the Manna, all that had been an easy method to clear the place out. So, no, I didn't want answers. I wanted them to stand face to face with me and know *I knew*.

Prior to the Morse code message, I'd not made assumptions. They could've been so alien that we wouldn't recognize each other as sentient. Or communication could prove impossible; they might talk in gassy expulsions or in weird finger gestures. But even then the torchships told me that wasn't likely. And, once I received the Morse message, I knew they were just like us. Oh, they could be bat-headed octopi but the basics of how they dealt with and understood the universe was enough like humanity's that we'd find a way.

The ship slid out of the sky, a rocket's dream of itself, shiny, sleek, and perfect. After it landed, a portal blossomed in the side and three creatures scuttled out. One was a small humanoid the size of a child's doll, paper white and peering with huge white eyes. The middle one looked like an ant mated with a fighter jet. It stood on six legs and a tear-shaped belly protruded straight up from its diminutive thorax. Atop the thorax a stalk held a bulb of eyes and tendrils. At the front of the thorax bobbed an aerodynamic head with a small mouth. Last, a bipedal robot ambled, with several arms and a head approximating a human in all the important details, made of plastic and ceramic. Something they built, I presumed, to make communication easier.

The two biological aliens masked their faces with breathing apparatus.

"Hello," I said.

The middle alien, the ant creature (huge, by the way, as big as a horse), leaned forward so its sensor stalk stretched down to me, all eyes and waving tendrils. The eyes blinked, uncannily human. The tendrils flashed with colors and thrummed until the robot piped up in perfect English.

"Hello. We have traveled a long time to meet you," it said.

"Why did you do it?" I asked.

The robot turned toward the middle alien and lights flashed from its face. The alien responded in kind.

"Many reasons for the departure from home system—"

"No, no, no, no. Why did you take Dad and Chase? Why the bread and the God stuff on TV?" My face felt warm and my eyes blurred. "I've lost everyone. They're all gone," And I cried. I sank to my knees and cried for a Heaven where I could see Mom again, and Dad. Where Chase and I could exchange rude comments and laughs. I cried for a universe where I couldn't see such a prospect as anything other than a nice story to tell children.

The small white alien came and gently placed a hand on my upper arm. We should have been too alien for either action to have any meaning, but they recognized sorrow, and I empathy. And from there we learned each other's stories.

For the past two years I have led the first human expedition on a jungle moon of one of Alpha Centauri Major's gas giants. I've marveled that what with Hubble and such we never saw a habitable planet in the closest solar system to home, but there you go.

The Piniom (the giant ant-like aliens) are hydrogen breathers. When their home system went through a technological singularity, the fleeing ships offered to bring members of the Tol race with them. The Tol lived underground on one of the moons orbiting the Piniom's gas giant.

The differing biologies alone convinced me they were not responsible for the Rapture. They came to beg use of the Jovian system. They could return to Alpha Centauri if need be. But they did not want to be alone.

So the children of humanity, and its religious rapture, and the children of the Eridani, and their tech singularity, found in each other a new family to hold close on the dark nights while we wonder what's out there that left us all behind.

Enough of us remained to carry on and to colonize a second world in a second solar system with the Piniom's help. Believers outnumber the agnostics and atheists. Folks who valued their faith over what they deemed a suspect offer of certainty. I've attended services that left me with tears in my eyes, wherein a reverend mother or pastor ironically referenced Einstein's quote about God not playing dice. But, in each service, they noted that God most definitely does not relieve us of our faith. It is a notion I'd like to believe Dad would have appreciated.

We have both more facts and more questions.

The life on the jungle moon is based on DNA. Though the plants and animals themselves are exotic and alien to us, they come from the same origins as earth life. And there is a Message *in* their DNA. The Tol and Piniom are based on a completely different set of building blocks. Not of the same origins, and lacking any tag set.

Would-be theologians among us argue they have no souls. It disappoints me.

My last days on earth I roamed the haunted streets and searched the buildings as they filled with tinkling music and echoes of laughter from farther rooms. I could hear trumpets and singing and out of the corners of my eyes, I might catch a flash of light. Walking in Dallas's downtown canyons, a warm wind sweeping trash down the street, a moment of immense calm beset me and I felt myself sinking into the city as though I was a building that would stand among the other buildings forever. The sun filled rectangles with neon umber along the flank of the great glass beast to my side. That feeling passed, and the colors around me grew more muted. I thought it from the coming twilight.

As the season passed and the first post-Rapture winter approached, the cities waxed pallid and buildings burgeoned as though alive with dream-born cancers. The cities came alive with lights in the night, and sounds like voices echoed in empty ruins.

Those who remained behind set to the task of understanding the metamorphosis of Earth's cities. They speculated some intelligence lingered in the transformed cities, belonging either to the raptured, or the agent of that rapture.

I'm going out to work on the Site Two excavation today. I sweat and strain on days like this. I worry about hurting myself as I grow old. But for the most part I enjoy the rays of the alien suns on my back and the feel of Laura beside me when she stops to bring me lunch and see how it's coming. She's the boss around here: I'm just the brawn. I'm going to have to let the younger ones handle this stuff pretty soon, though. I need to take care of Laura and myself.

I think back to all that I lost on Earth. Sometimes I guess we have to lose everything, even the certainties we always counted on.

There are hints of a long-dead civilization, and would-be xenologists (I am among these folks) speculate at a Rapture that came to this world when Earth was young and not yet home to sentience. It is bad science, I suspect, coming up with our conclusion and searching for evidence instead of the other way around, but there is time to introduce rigor to our methods and enthusiasm is its own reward.

We unearthed a pictogram today that my colleagues immediately interpreted to depict a Rapture event. I meant to ridicule them for jumping to conclusions, but instead I found myself chilled to the bone.

"Look there. It depicts awareness of the *Message* and first contact with aliens like our Piniom, missing a *Message*. And this here shows that they exist in simulation, as an intended civilization – hence the tag – and the aliens are an emergent civilization. Reasonable given the parameters necessary for the first—"

The team stared at me, shocked. It must have been a thought I'd held inside for some time, unexpressed even to myself. That old *Dickian* rationale holding on. Internally consistent. I shook my head and smiled.

"I'm not suggesting that's in fact what happened or what this depicts. I *am* pointing out why you can't start from a conclusion."

We returned to work and as time passes, my encouragement for rigor is making headway.

Sometimes, late at night, I wake up and I wonder.

I wish I could conclude this account with answers. I have no answers.

It doesn't matter if I am a created or a natural thing, or if the universe is a created or natural place. I am accountable to be the best man I can be. The rest is mystery, and living in mystery, seeking answers ... is the best definition I have for life.

And perhaps for faith.

Ever heard of Georges Lemaître? Almost a century ago, he earned a doctorate in physics and took holy orders as a Roman Catholic priest. Lemaître then did the seminal work which history has misidentified as "Hubble's law" and proposed the model of an expanding universe which detractors derisively labeled "the Big Bang theory." Yes, The Big Bang was conceived by a cleric who saw in it no inconsistency with the *Genesis* account of creation.

Today's religious leaders tend to ignore that. They might find other theories more palatable, though — for example, the proposition that the universe couldn't exist without an outside observer. Ultimately, there need not be an either/or dichotomy between science and spirituality. As for science and *faith*, though, maybe there's only room for one. Ian R. Thorpe takes us to the abandoned manor house in the English countryside where they collide.

A DIVINE LEGACY

IAN R. THORPE

"Go on Jester Jinks, go on my son!" a thin man at the wrong end of his thirties leaned forward in his chair as if riding to a finish himself, gesticulating wildly as the horse race he was yelling at on the television came to a climax. Dave's lank hair swung around his cheeks and his knees peeped through jeans that were more fatigued than fashionably distressed.

The horse he was cheering on, Jester Jinks, was ten lengths clear, approaching the final hurdle but suddenly seemed to lose concentration. Veering first to the right then the left, the animal completely forgot to check its stride and blundered into the hurdle, crashing down in a flurry of limbs while the jockey scrambled clear.

"Oh, for fuck's sake, you three-legged donkey, all you had to do was crawl over the hurdle and plod home."

This observation was a trifle superfluous because Jester Jinks was dead. Just as the unlucky punter was composing in his mind a rant against the capricious nature of Lady Luck in which, as he had so often before, he would dismiss that inconstant and capricious deity as no Lady but a cheap whore who had sold herself to the bookies once again. He was about to give voice to his emotions when the telephone rang.

"Loser," said the unlucky punter, not quite knowing whether he addressed the horse or himself, as he turned to pick up the telephone.

"Mister David Kidder," an unfamiliar voice said.

"Who wants to know?" Dave asked warily. He was not expecting any calls from a debt collector but it was always wise to be careful.

"My name is Gerald Creeme, I work for B.V. Heritage. Perhaps I ..."

"If you are from a charity, I'm on the dole. I have no money to spare for saving old buildings or buying art treasures and whatnot."

"I seem to have given you the wrong impression," Gerald said quickly before Dave had time to hang up. "What we do is help people claim money they are entitled to."

"Yeah, well we know our way round the benefits system so there's no point paying you a fee to do what we can do for ourselves, there's nothing we're not claiming."

"Mister Kidder, if you will let me finish please, our company's business is tracing the rightful heirs to estates that Her Majesty's Treasury has included on the *bona vacantia* list. That is ..."

"Yeah, yeah, like on that television programme in the mornings, *Heir Hunters*, I know about that. But nobody in my family died."

"If you watch the show you will know that many people we help are not aware they are due to inherit part of an estate, in fact quite a lot have never known of the relative from whom they are about to inherit. Anyway, at this stage I can't tell you if you are in line for an inheritance. We need to ask you a few questions and then confirm you are the right David Kidder."

Now Dave was all ears and very eager to meet Mr. Creeme.

The meeting was arranged for the following day. Dave had pushed for the first available appointment because he did not want to tell Demelza about the possible inheritance, but Mr. Creeme insisted he could not spare the time that afternoon. Dave cursed Lady Luck once again; if there had been any justice he would have found out how much, if anything, he stood to inherit while his partner was out at the Psychic Fair in town.

It wasn't that Dave did not care for Demelza, whose real name was Barbara but who knew people were more likely to part with money to have their palms or cards read by someone named Demelza, but that Dave was not into all the new age spirituality and life-is-a-quest stuff she was obsessed with. He could even put up with her vegetarianism so long as he could sneak off to Fat Andy's greasy spoon for a sausage sandwich or steak pie and chips while she was busy selling elixirs and potions at her stall in the flea market. Dave knew if he had a bit of money he could have fun – he could buy a classic motor bike, a minge-magnet sports car and maybe a quad bike. He could see his old mates and get drunk.

All the people Demelza knew were weirdie-beardies, sandal-wearing tree huggers whose idea of a good time was communicating with earth spirits.

A few weeks earlier Dave had gestured at the New Age artwork and spiritual symbols with which Demelza decorated their home (really her home because Dave had only been around four years), and told her it was all bollocks.

The fact that he had not backed a winner since that day had not penetrated his consciousness.

A silver car stopped outside the solid but slightly scruffy house, formerly a municipally owned property.

"So who's this guy again, Dave? He looks like an ex-copper. Are you sure he's not a debt collector or a bailiff?"

"He is from that programme on the telly, you know, where they trace long lost relatives of people who die without leaving a will. But he didn't say I deffo have something coming. They have to make enquiries first."

Demelza made a disdainful little noise and hurried to the door, anxious to let her psychic powers assess Mr. Creeme.

The meeting was friendly, although Dave thought Mr. Creeme was paying far more attention to Demelza's scoop neck T-shirt than was necessary. The business moved ahead however. Family documents including Dave's Australian birth certificate and things relating to his parents were examined; Gerald Creeme phoned his office and had intense conversations laden with legal jargon. Eventually he said, "I'm happy to tell you that we consider your case to be the sole heir of Charles Crozitter is proved and we will be happy to prosecute your claim ... for a commission of course."

"What do I stand to get?" Dave asked. "The name ain't even similar, so who was this geezer?"

"The actual monetary value realised when the Crown Solicitor sold Charles's personal effects was in the region of fifty thousand pounds. Our commission, should you engage us to process the claim, is twenty percent. There are also certain administrative charges so you would get about thirty-five thousand."

"Thirty-five ... that's robbery! I'll process the claim myself."

"That's your prerogative, but you would have to pay your own legal fees and you are by no means certain to win the case. And of course, other heirs may come forward. We work on a no win, no fee basis."

"It still sounds like a con."

"Listen to the man," Demelza said sharply. Her instinct told her Gerald was a bit of a smoothie, but basically OK. "We could even end up owing money if we go it alone, and how often are we going to get a chance of picking up thirty-five thousand pounds?"

"Give or take a few hundred," Gerald interjected. His instinct had told him Demelza was the intelligent one. And he liked her slightly slutty Goth look.

"OK," said Dave, "we'll sign up. Like Demmy says, thirty-five grand is not to be sneezed at."

"Quite, but there's more. Here's what makes this such an interesting estate. The monetary value is unspectacular but there is a property too that is part of the legacy and it is difficult to put a value on that as things stand. Charles Crozitter was the last of the very ancient Croix de Guerre family. The name became corrupted over the years to become Crozitter and Kidder respectively.

"He's called Kidder because he's never taken anything like work seriously in his life," Demelza said, throwing Gerald a flirtatious look.

Gerald laughed and carried on explaining the legal process that would be set in train once Dave signed the form appointing B.V. Heritage as his agents.

"The term *bona vacantia* literally means 'vacant goods' and is the legal name for ownerless property, which by law passes to the Crown," said the man from The Treasury Solicitor's Office. "Naturally it would cause a bit of a furore if Her Maj's men just grabbed all unclaimed property after the statutory ten years has elapsed. So depending on the size and nature of the estate, we publish a list of *bona vacantia* on the first of the month and allow a variable amount of time for claimants to come forward."

Mr. Baring, the man from the Treasury Solicitor's Office droned on, obviously relishing the technical details of the case; next to him Gerald Creeme admired the scenery as they drove towards Dave's inheritance. In the back seat of the car Dave and Demelza tried to make each other laugh. They were as excited as children about to set out on a treasure hunt, having been told the substantial property included a manor house, a medieval chapel and some land. Demelza had been particularly excited to hear there was a stone circle on the land.

Dave was already planning to turn the manor house into apartments, which he thought would sell at about quarter of a million pounds each, and to sell the fifty acres of land for housing development; building land in the area was fetching around £400,000 an acre he had heard.

"That's er ... umm ... a lot of money," he had told Demelza but she was thinking in terms of turning the medieval chapel into a pagan centre and using the stone circle as the centerpiece for a folk and majick festival.

As the car stopped Gerald slid out and went to open a gate that blocked the dirt track they had driven on for the past quarter mile. Mr. Baring announced the main property would be visible once they cleared a stretch of woodland just beyond the gate.

"Shall we leave the car and walk from here?" Demelza's tone made it clear her question was a command.

"A good idea," the civil servant said and began to get out of the car as Gerald closed the gate.

The walk through the wood took about three minutes at an easy pace and, as they walked, the Treasury Solicitor's man chattered about the unique nature of the legacy.

"The manor house is one of the oldest in England. It was the scene of a skirmish in the Civil War when the owner, a Royalist, held out for several months against the Parliamentarians. Of course it fell into disrepair in the mid-nineteenth century when Nathaniel Crozitter, son of Tubalcain, found that his ancestor, who founded the estate, was a Knight Templar and uncovered an old family legend that the Crusader had brought back a priceless treasure from The Holy Land. He spent a fortune on trying to discover what the treasure was and where it was hidden. It was even rumoured The Ark Of The Covenant is somewhere on the estate. There is a passage in the will of Tubalcain Crozitter that refers to it but unfortunately the wording is rather obscure. Roughly translated, it reads, 'In the temple is the thing of greatest value. Here is the greatest prize of Croix de Guerre. Here is the wisdom of Hermes Trismegistus, which opens for him who possesses it understanding of all things.

Whoever holds this knowledge will know the truth of all things, have mastery of the world and will speak with God'."

"Unfortunately Nathaniel misunderstood and worked on the assumption that great power and wealth would come to whoever solved the puzzle, whereas it probably means great wisdom and understanding."

It was Demelza who spoke first, before Dave could ask what this priceless thing might fetch at auction.

"Hermes Trismegistus, thrice master, was the god of Tyre, a Phoenician deity. He's mixed up with Freemasonry and Zoroastrianism. Hey, this could be talking about the green tablet of Hermes that was once owned by Isaac Newton. This is fascinating."

As she spoke they rounded a bend and saw before them the legacy.

"It's beautiful," Demelza said.

"It's a ruin, a fucking ruin." Dave wailed in despair, as somewhere deep in his inner being he sensed the scornful laughter of Lady Luck.

The old house was both beautiful and a ruin. Parts of the roof had gone and the sunlight shining through some of the mullioned windows, came from inside the house and fell on those standing outside. Buddleia and willow herb grew from the gutters and brickwork, windows that were still intact were opaque with grime. The place may have been decaying beautifully but it was decaying expensively. The west wing, the last part of the old house to have been inhabited, was in better condition but was still clearly not fit for habitation.

Demelza was enchanted and already planning her pagan festival that would be held at the site every year.

Dave clutched at straws.

"I suppose we could demolish it and sell the land for building, that would raise some money," he said hopefully.

"I'm afraid not," said Mr. Baring. "It's a Grade One listed building. You would have to spend a fortune in legal fees to have a chance of getting it delisted."

"What about converting to apartments?"

This time Gerald burst his bubble.

"Listed building you can only restore to the original condition."

"Well, what about if we fence off the building and sell the land?"

"You could perhaps sell it for grazing but that would not raise much and the farming industry has been hit by the debt crisis. Better to rent it perhaps and get a bit of regular income. It's green belt you see, land reserved for agriculture."

"Yes, and there are the two ancient monuments on it, the medieval chapel and the stone circle, they're round the other side of the house," Mr. Baring said, sounding much happier than he needed to. "Also that wooded area we walked through is designated ancient woodland. That's protected by law too."

Dave was thinking that Lady Luck was no ordinary whore, she was an S&M queen.

Noticing his client was looking downcast, Gerald said, "There is of course the treasure in the chapel. Mister Baring has asked someone from English Heritage along to explain the historical aspects of the legacy. The man should be here soon."

"Did you say a stone circle?" Demelza asked, her eyes alight with excitement. Gerald had only seen a photograph of the circle but found it easy to imagine the dark-haired woman dancing naked among the stones.

They waited until the representative from English Heritage arrived riding a mountain bike and wearing a helmet which, when he dismounted, made him look like a penguin with its head on backwards.

"Greetings," he said extending his hand, "My name is Julian Dickey. Shall we take the full tour?"

It would be, Dickey by name and dicky by nature, Dave thought.

After handshakes and introductions they set of to walk round the outside of the house. It was a sprawling old manor that had been built in bits, the earliest parts dating back to the thirteenth century with other sections in various styles added on. The west wing was as recent as the mid-eighteenth century.

"And as we round this corner you will see the chapel," Julian Dickey announced as if reciting a tour itinerary.

"Wow!" Demelza exclaimed as the medieval church came into view, "I'm getting such good vibes from this place. The medieval church in England was much closer to the pagan roots of Christianity than modern religion. They really understood the mysteries then."

"Bollocks," Dave mumbled.

He thought he had uttered the curse under his breath but Julian Dickey said, "Not at all! Demelza is absolutely right. Take the story of Mary Gypsy or Mary the Egyptian to whom this chapel is dedicated. It is full of Druidic symbolism."

"Moon worship and such," said Gerald Creeme, who was walking a couple of paces behind them so he could appreciate the way Demelza's shapely bottom moved seductively under the thin material of her ethnic print skirt.

"We can look inside in just a moment but first round this corner we come to the stone circle. It is not very grand compared with Stonehenge or Avebury but the proximity of the Christian chapel and the pagan place of worship are interesting. Here you see, one of the standing stones has actually been incorporated in the cornerpiece of the church."

Mr. Baring was surprisingly knowledgeable on the significance of the church's sacred architecture as well as the Druidic sacred geometry of the stone circle intersecting, and went on to discuss the purpose of pagan symbolism in Christian art. When Julian joined in on the theme, the others were sidelined for a few minutes.

As the civil servant and the historian talked, Dave wandered off to try to discern what the interior of the ancient church might hold, his girlfriend surveyed the stone circle and the architecture of the church, seeing all sorts of pagan symbolism in the two and Gerald took the opportunity to say, in a whisper, "I think your boyfriend is looking for a quick buck and missing the potential of this place."

"You mean as a, like, pagan retreat or something? Chilltastic."

"That is one idea certainly, but this needs to be thought through properly. I looked up the ancient property deeds last time I was in the area. Can you see that clump of trees down the slope there?" Her eye followed the direction of his pointing finger. "There is a well house built over a spring, said to be sacred to the people who built this stone circle."

"It gets better and better," Demelza said.

"We've hardly started," Gerald assured her. "We must arrange to talk privately because we are obviously thinking on the same lines."

Demelza reached into her bag, fumbled around and then handed the inheritance chaser a card advertising her services as a teller of fortunes and psychic healer. Just as the man was tucking it into his shirt pocket, the others broke off their private conversation and announced it was time to enter the church. While

Julian opened the door, Dave muttered glumly about not expecting to find anything of value inside.

The interior of the old building was something of a shock. It seemed much larger than it had looked from outside. The sacred architecture was devised to produce that impression by a trick of light and proportion, but the vaulted ceiling and the way the pillars tapered gave the impression that the roof was pulling the rest of the building upwards.

"Since the beginnings of civilization humans have constructed monuments to, for want of a better term, a divine ideal. Stone circles, Jewish, Hindu and Zoroastrian temples, cathedrals and mosques have all been constructed to represent the sacred and ineffable qualities of the universe in their structure. They are beacons of spiritual energy that call to the human soul to return to the original source of unity and wholeness. There are modern and ancient books on sacred architecture that trace the history of this creative human impulse and the way it records our relationship with the Divine, God if you like, from early prehistoric cultures to contemporary times and these highlight a consistent theme."

Julian spoke with his usual enthusiasm and Dave stifled a yawn.

The chapel burst with ancient symbols and weird patterns carved in the stone but nobody could see any clue to the priceless treasure referred to in the old wills. Demelza took photographs and made notes and sketches of everything in the chapel. She was aware that a priceless treasure to people in the medieval era might have no commercial value at all in the twenty-first century. The well house, away down the slope, was equally mysterious, with pagan symbols including a wheel whose spokes were made from a lion, a goat, an eagle and a man. Above the place where the two springs bubbled up into a small stone reservoir, was a niche designed to hold a light of some sort. Again there were no explanations readily available.

"There is something else you must see inside the main house, but we should not really go in without hard hats," Julian Dickey told them. After a quick discussion it emerged that Gerald had a couple of safety helmets in the back of his car, as he often had to go into long-unoccupied buildings; Julian carried his own cycling helmet and a spare.

The rooms of the west wing were faded and dusty but, apart from a few places on the upper floor where leaks in the roof had caused damage, it was quite impressive. The thing Julian had spoken of was at the topmost level of the house, a turret or tower added on after the rest of the building had matured.

"It says in this book, *A History of Croix de Guerre Hall and Surroundings*, this turret was added in the eighteenth century by Tubalcain Crozitter, who was an explorer in Egypt and the Middle East. On his return from an expedition, he took an avid interest in the mysteries of the Hermetics. He was following in the footsteps of Isaac Newton of course, but the man who wrote this history thinks he had also discovered something about his ancestor Gilles Croix de Guerre, a Knight Templar by all accounts. Now I've been up here before but when the rest of you see it, you will be astounded."

The reaction fell a little short of Julian's expectations because none of the others knew what they were looking at in the turret at the top of the house. It looked like a room with a domed ceiling on which a map of the night sky had been painted.

A passage in the history book revealed it to be much more than that. What the eighteenth-century seeker of truth had constructed was an astrolabe or planetarium. The whole ceiling of the room was a working model of the stars in the northern sky. Most ancient astrolabes had been clockwork but moved by hand, the mechanism geared to reproduce the movements of the stars. Tubalcain Crozitter had caused water to be ducted through the cellars to drive a mechanism similar to a medieval water clock, and connected to the astrolabe in the roof by a series of metal shafts and gear wheels.

By an ingenious system, a multi-layered model moved the planets and constellations exactly as the stars in the real sky moved.

"I don't know about priceless, but this must be worth a lot of money to the right buyer, the science museum or Bill Gates or somebody," Dave speculated only to be told that the preservation orders would prevent its being tampered with, even if removing it was technically feasible.

"Wait, look at this!" Demelza shouted as the party turned to leave. She was looking at the pictures in the playback feature of her digital camera. Julian and Gerald asked what she had seen. Mr. Baring looked interested, Dave sighed.

"These three constellations," she pointed to clusters of dots on the ceiling, "they are represented by their symbols above the three vertical windows behind the altar in the chapel."

"And?" asked Dave as the others moved to look at the image in the LCD window of Demelza's camera.

"It's a clue. Whatever the secret is, wherever it is hidden, there will be clues to help the enlightened find it."

"I'm rather good at crosswords and Sudoku if that's any help," Mr. Baring offered.

"Probably a big help, but you haven't told us your first name yet," Demelza scolded him. Having learned he was named John, the four people who were fascinated by the challenge set about trying to understand what the puzzle they hoped to solve might be. Dave, frustrated that nobody was interested in talking about how he might turn his inheritance into cash, slumped on the floor.

As the others were enthusing about a small reproduction of William Blake's painting *The Ancient of Days* found near the bottom of a segment in the domed ceiling, Dave announced he was going to wait by the car. Once outside and away from the surveillance of Village Green Preservation Society, the biker took out his cell phone, used its internet feature to look up a number and placed a call to the office of Rex Trevor, a press agent who had obtained fortunes for glamour models who had been bedded by politicians, footballers wives and girlfriends who wanted to expose their partners as serial cheats, and celebrities who wanted to revive flagging careers through confessional tales of their descent into a drink and drugs hell.

"You've inherited the Holy Grail, you say?" The woman speaking to Dave had an upper-crust accent and the pushiness of someone who thought she deserved more limelight than could ever come from being a press agent's assistant. She had introduced herself as Jemima Bradley-Parker and the voice suited the hyphenated name.

"Not exactly," Dave hedged. "I mean, we know I have but there are a few clues to solve before we actually find it. It might be in the old manor house, the medieval chapel or the well house built over the Druids' sacred wells."

"So what's the story? I mean, it sounds great for you but we have to have a story to sell."

"Well, my other half and the guy from English Heritage are keen to keep this quiet. The Holy Grail, everybody is interested in that story. Even I read *The Da Vinci Code*. I thought it was shite, mind."

"So you think the authorities will try to cover up the knowledge of this?"

"Too bloody right. I mean, why does nobody know about this

place? It should be right up there with Stonehenge, Rosslyn Chapel, The Temple Church and Glastonbury."

"I see what you mean, OK, yeah, get us some details and photos, e-mail them to us and we'll find an angle,"

"I'm not in it just for the money you know," Dave said, "for me it's about reclaiming Britain's spiritual heritage – King Arthur and stuff."

"Yeah, right," said Jemima. "Get that material to us as soon as you can."

Dave travelled back to Starkbridge alone. His lady had decided to spend the next two days in the area trying to unravel the secrets held by the mysterious symbols and artefacts of Croix de Guerre Manor. As it happened, Gerald had business in the area and offered to pay for her to stay at the small, comfortable hotel he used.

After two days frantic research, helped by Julian Dickey, Demelza had found that the symbols and the astrolabe told an ancient myth, the marriage of heaven and earth which featured in the traditions of most ancient societies. It was an allegory for how God or the gods had come down to earth, lifted humans from the darkness of unconsciousness and set them on the path to enlightenment. She had also enjoyed two excellent dinners, followed by drinks in the bar and intimate conversations in a more private setting with Gerald and revealed she had only become Dave's wife because he had never applied for a work permit after forgetting to go home to Australia. It settled a possible legal problem.

After booking another night in the hotel Gerald drove his new paramour to the manor where Julian Dickey was waiting, and then set off to chase down more inheritors, promising to be back as soon as he could.

Julian was almost as excited as Demelza. He too felt his research had yielded something important.

"The Green Tablet of Hermes is legendary," he announced. "It is said to have once been in the possession of Isaac Newton, who was a friend of Simon Croix de Guerre in the seventeenth century – and I think we might be very close to it now."

"The star signs and symbols point to a location in the chapel that relates to those three windows," Demelza offered, not wishing to be outdone. "The message seems to be saying the chapel is somehow a conduit between Earth and the heavens, specifically Orion's belt."

They went to the chapel and looked in the locations indicated by Tubalcain Crozitter's documents. It did not take long to find a panel on the wall that was easily removed. Behind the stone plaque was a niche in which lay an emerald-green crystal tablet. Beneath it was a piece of parchment.

"It's Greek. That's lucky – I did Greek at school. We should not have to send it off to be translated."

Dave used a bread roll to mop the gravy from a plate as the tabloid reporter reviewed his notes. The biker was grateful that Demelza's enthusiasm for the project had led her to upload her photographs via smartphone and notes to her web site. He had known his wife's password for a long time, proving she was wise in not fully trusting him. With the pictures and notes, Rex Trevor had worked quickly and efficiently, using phrases like "Holy Grail", "Messages from God" and "Ark Of The Covenant" to sensationalize the story. After a brief auction, Dave agreed to give the *Daily Stirrer* an exclusive. The *Stirrer's* readers loved a conspiracy story and the way the secrets of the Manor had been kept under wraps was a gem.

Two hours away, across the country, Julian Dickey and Demelza were growing impatient with Gerald's attempts to start a conversation as, with the aid of a newly purchased Greek-English dictionary, they laboriously translated the text of the Green tablet.

It was a long night but eventually they had something.

"It doesn't make much sense," said Julian. "This stuff about 'bread of heaven,' that's a well-known hymn. But what is it doing here? It suggests the tablet is a fake."

"Not really. The phrase was used by alchemists to mean white powder gold, a substance created by somehow rearranging the orbit of electrons in gold atoms. The substance was said to have amazing healing and antigravity properties, which enabled ancient builders to hoist massive stones in temples and monuments to incredible heights."

"But how could the ancients know about that?" Gerald asked.

"How did they know about electricity?" Demelza matched question with question. "But the Ark of the Covenant was a heavy-duty capacitor. And did you know, with the best modern technology we could not recreate the Pyramids or Solomon's Temple? So how did they do it five thousand years ago?"

It seemed the secrets of the Croix de Guerre family were closely connected with all this.

Next morning at the manor, the first stop was the well house. The parchment from the chapel indicated a cartouche between two mythical creatures carved in bas-relief. When given a good bash with the heel of Gerald's hand, it caused one of the bas-reliefs to move forward slightly. Pulling the stone out of its setting revealed a metal oval with a black, gemstone-cut cabochon. Pressing this caused the whole rear wall of the well house to move.

Just then Gerald's phone rang. Hearing half of the conversation, his companions could tell it was not good news.

"The papers said what? They're what? It can't be! We don't know what we've found yet and, no, I haven't come over all *Da Vinci Code*. Thanks for letting us know."

"That dickhead has blabbed to the tabloids, I said he was after a quick buck. The paparazzi and the media dogs are on their way."

"He said you were after a quick shag," Demelza said, pushing her hip against his. "What are we going to do?"

Gerald said he'd fix it, then called the chief constable of the county police.

"What are we the same distance from?" he asked.

"From the centre, brother," was the reply. Gerald explained quickly what was happening and warned the mob was likely to tear the place apart. He ended the call and told the others his brother mason was arranging a police presence.

The site was secured minutes before media laid siege to the place. With officers outside, the seekers were able to venture into the subterranean chamber behind the well house. Again the text on the green tablet yielded clues, Tubalcain Crozitter had faithfully reproduced something long lost to humanity.

"Cross the river of life and partake of the bread of heaven. Then drink from the waters and behold the face and hear the voice of the Divine," the tablet had instructed. The river was a still pool filled with the water that flowed into the well house. They picked their way over stepping stones to a platform where, on a stone plinth was a small pile of white powder. The heavy-looking stone plinth wobbled at each light touch.

"Is that made of Styrofoam?" Gerald asked. Julian took hold

of it, pronounced it real, and lifted it with ease. Then he took away his hands and to everyone's amazement the plinth remained twelve inches above the floor.

When they had each placed a pinch of the powder on their tongue and washed it down with a handful of water from the pool, their perception immediately changed. It was as if they had risen to the top of the chamber and were looking down on the pool. And though it was morning outside, in the water were reflected the stars of the night sky.

"Are you sure that was powder gold and not powdered mushrooms?" Gerald asked. "But those stars aren't a reflection on the surface. They're in the depths of the pool."

"'Shrooms wouldn't work that quick and the sensation is not like speed or coke," Demelza said, sounding as if she knew about such things.

"How is the night sky visible in the depths of the pool, when the roof of this place is solid and it's daytime outside?" Julian wanted to know.

Gerald called on his Masonic knowledge. "There are beliefs about a Biblical character called Tubalcain and this white powder gold stuff," he said, "But nobody ever really understood them. This stuff is supposed to transcend the physical constraints of the universe, to put us in contact with other dimensions beyond time and space. Now look into the depths of the pool again. Is it a reflection of the astrolabe?"

Demelza said it was not, the constellations were in the wrong positions. They looked deeper into the still water to the chapel ceiling also reflected in the depths. Julian spoke excitedly of quantum entanglements theory and said many academics thought modern physics was barking up the wrong tree.

"Everything is connected with everything else. We could never understand the nature of the universe because we are part of it," he said, "and the tablet tells us how to make the powder gold that puts us outside the laws of physics."

"My God, I think we have just found proof that God exists," Gerald stuttered. "The white powder has placed us outside the dimensions of time and space. We are looking outside time and space, looking in."

"And everything is part of a whole, a consciousness. This is going to change everything," Demelza said.

"Do you think people will believe it?" Gerald asked, "They want certainties, Big Daddy looking after them. This will go down well with the freethinkers and we can do well out of them, but for most people it will change nothing."

Inherent in the proposition of a Judeo-Christian God is that He is not only omnipotent, but also beneficent. Inherent in the "Christian" end of that hyphen is that there exists a malevolent being who has rebelled against God. From there we could get into the morass of why an all-powerful deity who is conceived of as a loving parent or shepherd would permit such shenanigans. We *could*, but we won't.

Instead, we offer this short, light-hearted tale from James Hartley, who observes how Orlando can be mistaken for Heaven, and airline travel can be mistaken for Hell. And how, if there is a God, each of us – no matter our foibles – is a part of His plan.

ACCIDENT PRONE

JAMES HARTLEY

When Sid looked down from the plane window he saw angels skiing on the cloud banks below. Up until then the flight had been normal. Well, at least as normal as anything ever was in Sid's accident prone life, but this was unusual even for Sid.

Sid's taxi had gotten a flat tire on the way to the airport and he had arrived at the terminal barely on time. The girl behind the counter had been most unpleasant about it, and Sid blamed that aggravation for the fainting spell at the security checkpoint. He had experienced a sudden sharp pain in his chest and blacked out.

When he came to, he was sitting on the floor looking up at several airport attendants. One of them was asking, "How are you feeling? Are you OK? Should we call for an ambulance?" Several of them helped him to his feet, and the one who had been asking the questions took his ticket and inspected it. Handing it back to Sid, he said, "I'm certainly glad you're feeling better, Mister Herbert, but it's a good thing I checked. You were heading for the wrong gate."

"Wrong gate?" protested Sid. He looked down at the ticket, and then up at the sign on the wall, wondering what was wrong this time. The numbers seemed to match. "No, look here. My ticket says Gate 84, flight 721 to Orlando. And the sign over there says Gates 81 to 90. This is my gate." But inside he had the usual sinking feeling. Probably the girl had written one thing and said something different, or the computer printed the wrong thing. Or the sign painter had mislabeled the corridor. Sure, why not?

The attendant, who wore a badge bearing the name 'Michael' surrounded by a pair of feathery wings, nodded his head. "Yes, sir, but there has been a change. If you would care to look for yourself?" He pointed at a bank of TV monitors listing departures. The line for flight 721 to Orlando said 'Gate 84', but as Sid watched, the '84' faded out and was replaced by '1000'.

"Gate 1000? Gate 1000? I've been in this airport hundreds of times, and I never heard of a Gate 1000." Sid could count the number of times he had actually flown on the fingers of one hand, but he had been in the airport hundreds of times. Waiting for flights canceled due to weather. Waiting for flights canceled due to engine trouble. Waiting for overbooked flights where he was always the one bumped, and somehow he never got any compensation. Sid had wandered the corridors of the airport from one end to the other, and he had never seen a gate number higher than 99. "Is Gate 1000 new?"

"No, sir, Gate 1000 has been around for a long time. A very long time." The attendant firmly but gently took Sid's arm and led him to a moving walkway. "Just go down this slidewalk, and when you come to a branch in the corridor, go right for Gate 1000. Be sure not to go left, that leads to Gate 666, and we wouldn't want to go there, now, would we, sir?" He chuckled as if sharing a joke with Sid, but Sid didn't have the faintest idea what he was talking about.

The attendant applied gentle pressure to Sid's arm, and Sid found himself moving down the slidewalk. A slidewalk, he noted mentally, that he had never seen, or at least never noticed, before this. Sure enough, there was a branch, and he followed instructions and went right, down another corridor to Gate 1000. At the end of this one was the usual waiting room full of chairs, but the girl at the desk waved him right through the door into the plane. He just had time to stow his bag and his jacket in the overhead compartment and take his seat before the pilot started to taxi.

From that point on, the flight was ordinary enough. They ran out of Coke one seat before they got to him, and he had to drink ginger ale, but at least there were enough meals. On a previous flight, he had gone hungry when they ran out. The flight remained ordinary until he looked down from the plane window and saw angels skiing on the cloud banks below.

Sid tried to tell the stewardess about the skiing angels, but just then the pilot announced that they were making their approach, and everyone was busy.

Sid checked his watch, as it seemed too early to have arrived at Orlando, but it had stopped, probably when he blacked out and fell. He looked out the window again, but now all he could see was clouds. Then, as the plane banked around for its approach, he saw the airport in the distance. It didn't look much like Orlando. Sid gave a sigh of resignation at the thought of ending up in the wrong city, and wondered where he was. This airport looked bigger than Orlando's, much, much bigger. And it was a funny color, sort of gold.

He watched out the window as they approached. They were only feet off the ground when suddenly the plane's engines revved up to full speed and they started to climb. A 'go-round', something blocking the runway. It hardly ever happened, they said, but it had happened on every flight Sid had ever taken. They made a big circle around the airport, giving Sid a better look, and on the second attempt they managed to land. After they had taxied to a stop, Sid took his coat and bag from the overhead storage and walked to the exit.

As he came out of the boarding ramp into the gate area, Sid paused and looked around. This was definitely not Orlando. Everything was done in an iridescent white luster. Sid walked across the waiting area and was about to go looking for the baggage claim when he noticed two men arguing. With a start he realized that one was the airport attendant named Michael he had left behind in the other airport, but now wearing a pilot's uniform. The other man had a similar badge, with the name 'Peter' flanked by the feathery wings, but his badge also had a narrow ellipse over the name. The two men were making no attempt to conceal their argument, so Sid stopped to listen.

"What in Cosmos happened on that landing, Michael? Why did you pull up suddenly at the last minute? Things like that make havoc of our schedules, as well as frightening the passengers."

"Don't blame me. It was the tower that called for a go-round. I was just following orders. The tower says go-round, I go-round."

"But don't you realize? That was the first go-round that has ever happened here. Something is wrong, seriously wrong. Perhaps the Adversary is getting a clawhold. We have to do something ..." Peter's voice trailed off as he spotted Sid. He turned, suddenly all smiles, and said, "Welcome, Mister Herbert. We're glad to have you here with us."

Sid looked at him nervously. Glad-handers were one of his worst jinxes, they always triggered some sort of trouble. But he needed a few answers. "Thank you, but where are we? This doesn't look like Orlando."

"Well, no, Mister Herbert, this isn't Orlando. Just look around you," he said, waving his hand at the area in which they stood, and then at hundreds of similar areas up and down the corridor, all built from the same lustrous white material. "Don't you recognize the Pearly Gates?"

Sid started. "You mean I'm, I'm, I'm ... dead? This is Heaven?"

"Yes, of course, Mister Herbert. Welcome to Heaven. I'm sure you'll enjoy it."

Peter's voice stopped suddenly as a huge piece of the pearly wall came loose and fell on him with a loud crash, just missing Sid. "Oh, Cosmos!" came a muffled curse from under the block, and then the piece of wall floated up to its previous spot. Peter stood there, unharmed. He gave Sid a long, searching look, and then, motioning Sid to wait, he went over to a nearby computer terminal and started typing. He spent several minutes at this, his frown deepening as he read. Finally he took a sheet of paper from the printer and came back to Sid. "Mr. Herbert," he said, "I'm afraid there has been a mistake. Your unfortunate condition, your accident proneness, is a definite symptom of Original Sin. It's not your fault, but we can't have you here. You'll have to go to The Other Place."

The Other Place! Sid shivered at the thought. Being dead was bad enough, but to have to go down into eternal torture? "Wait a minute," he said. "If it's not my fault, why should I have to suffer? Can't I file an appeal, or something?"

"Mr. Herbert, I know it's very hard to understand, but here in Heaven we pride ourselves on perfection. Perfection is our main weapon against the Adversary. You, on the other hand, spread imperfection with your accident proneness. If we allow you to remain, we weaken ourselves in the eternal struggle."

Peter had left his pencil sitting on top of the terminal. Now, suddenly, the pencil rolled down the sloping top and into a ventilation opening. There was a bright flash and a loud pop, and the terminal began to emit clouds of dense black smoke. Peter slapped the off switch and grabbed a fire extinguisher.

When the fire was out, Peter wiped his forehead and turned back to Sid. "You see what you're doing to us, Mister Herbert? No, you must go. Quickly, please." Peter took Sid's arm and walked him to a large elevator. There was only one button, marked 'Down', and Peter reached in through the door and pressed it. As the doors closed Sid tried to jump back out, but he found his muscles wouldn't obey him and he was unable to move. The elevator started to sink.

After a long time, it could have been minutes or hours or even days, the elevator stopped and the doors opened. Sid stepped out and found himself in a hotel lobby, facing a sign that read 'Hotel Brimstone'. Sid walked straight ahead toward the registration desk. Of course the clerk, a slender man with tiny bumps on either side of his forehead, was very busy shuffling papers behind the counter, and managed to ignore Sid for almost ten minutes. Anyone else might have given up and gone away, but for Sid a mere ten-minute wait was good service.

Finally the clerk, realizing that Sid was not going to leave, put down his stack of papers and said, "Can I help you, sir?"

"I just got here. I was sent down by Peter, and I have no idea where I should go or anything. My name is Herbert, Sid Herbert."

"Oh, yes, Mister Herbert. We received a message about your arrival. You'll be in room 1313. The maid is just making it up – it will be ready in an eon or two. Just have a seat in the lobby and we'll page you when it's ready."

The clerk waved Sid toward a row of uncomfortable-looking wooden benches.

Sid went over and started to sit down on one as directed, but somehow his foot became entangled in the legs of the bench and he upset it, dumping the occupants to the floor. Instead of scattering across the room, however, they all rolled on top of the large demon in the center and knocked him unconscious by the sheer weight of numbers. Then, realizing that the demon was no longer guarding them, the former occupants of the bench got up and scurried out the door.

The desk clerk pushed the alarm button, but at the first strike of the hammer, the gong shattered with a loud crack, leaving the hammer to vibrate back and forth silently. The clerk grabbed the phone but that was dead too. He threw the useless phone down and came running around the end of the desk, but he slipped on a small throw rug, fell to the floor, and knocked himself out. Sid, still trying to extricate his foot from the legs of the bench, watched in amazement. He was used to accidents happening around him, but this series of events was the worst he had ever seen. He shook his head and waited to see what would happen next.

He didn't have long to wait. One wall of the lobby collapsed revealing a swimming pool filled with molten brimstone, and millions immersed in it up to their necks. The three sides away from him were completely enclosed, but the nearest side was just a low wall. Guard demons patrolled the wall, prodding with their pitchforks any damned souls that approached too closely to the open side and freedom.

The upper stories of the hotel were disintegrating now, and a large hunk of debris fell right on the edge of the pool, cracking the wall. A stream of molten brimstone squirted out and struck one of the demons a terrific blow in the chest, knocking him backwards out of sight. The crack widened to a gap, then progressed in either direction until the entire wall was gone. The resulting tidal wave of brimstone washed all the guard demons under the lobby of the hotel, but somehow didn't affect the souls in the pit. As the level of lava got down to their ankles, they turned and ran toward and through the back wall of the pool.

Sid was flabbergasted. He had never seen such a collection of disasters. Was this simply his accident proneness, or was it something to do with the place in which he found himself? All at once, there was an even louder noise and the entire hotel collapsed around him, leaving him standing on one tiny bit of intact floor in a sea of rubble and debris.

He looked around and realized that the area of destruction was widening, a vast expanding circle around him collapsing into shards and dust. The sky was filled with thousands and millions of damned souls making their escape as the guard demons were caught in the undertow of destruction. In one direction, the tide of brimstone was lapping at the feet of an immense black iron castle. The castle itself was beginning to shake, but from the castle a more than humanly powerful voice said "Enough!" and everything froze.

Standing on the balcony of the castle was a giant man, somehow both bright red and inky black at the same time, with huge horns on his head and a long pointed tail. He was surrounded by a dozen or so of the guard demons. He looked around at the ruins of his domain, and finally his eyes fell on Sid. "Who are you?" he asked.

Sid looked around, but there was nobody else for miles. Realizing that the being was talking to him, he replied, "I'm Sid. Sid Herbert."

"You will address me as 'Sire', or as 'Your Foulness', worm, or suffer the consequences. Tell me, what are you doing here?"

"Yes, Your Foulness, Sire," quavered Sid. "I was in Heaven, but things started to go wrong, so Peter sent me down here. Something about original sin, and how I was destroying their perfection, and I couldn't stay there. He put me on the elevator down to the hotel. I've always been accident prone, Sire, but nothing like this. Things just started to collapse around me."

"Silence!" thundered the giant being. Then, in a more conversational tone, "Original Sin, my cloven hoof! Peter never was very smart about these things. Original Chaos is more like it. You're cursed with a touch of what was there before the Seven Days. On earth, or in Heaven, the orderliness of Creation keeps it in check. But down here things are a lot looser, and well, you see what has happened. Millions of damned souls escaped, and probably saved by now. The whole place a wreck! It will take eight or ten eons just to rebuild the brimstone pool! No, you can't stay here!"

Sid considered this, then asked, "But Your Foulness, if I can't be in Heaven and I can't be in Hell, what's left?"

"Silence!" The giant raised his pitchfork and sent a ray of searing redness upward into the void. After a short time, a beam of equally searing white lanced downward, then merged with the red to form a golden tube of energy connecting Hell with Heaven for only the third time since the Fall. Satan spoke, and

Sid could hear whispers of a voice replying from the other end. Sid wondered if it was Peter or perhaps even Peter's Boss, but he was afraid to ask. After an indeterminable amount of time, the conversation ended and the golden tube vanished. The giant demon aimed His pitchfork at Sid, and again the searing red ray leapt forth. Before Sid could even think about trying to duck, he was enveloped in a universe of red, and then all went black.

Sid's taxi had gotten a flat tire on the way to the airport, and he had arrived at the terminal barely on time. The girl behind the counter had been most unpleasant about it, and Sid blamed that aggravation for the fainting spell at the security checkpoint. He had experienced a sudden sharp pain in his chest and almost blacked out.

A courteous airport attendant whose name badge read 'Michael' noticed his discomfort and gave him a ride out to the gate in a little electric cart, but even so he was delayed, and when he got there all the other passengers had already boarded.

They were just about to close the door, but the girl at the desk waved him through into the plane. He just had time to stow his bag and his jacket in the overhead compartment and take his seat before the pilot started to taxi out to the runway.

From that point on, the flight was ordinary enough. They ran out of Coke one seat before they got to him, and he had to drink ginger ale, but at least there were enough meals. On a previous flight, before he had gone hungry when they ran out. The flight remained ordinary all the way to Orlando. Sid looked out of the window once in a while, but all he saw were clouds, ordinary clouds.

The plane landed at Orlando, but not without a go-round. As

Sid disembarked, he saw two men arguing about the landing. One of them, the pilot, had a name badge reading 'Michael', and Sid thought he looked a lot like the other Michael who had given him the ride out to the gate. Sid wondered if he had somehow acquired a guardian angel, but then he laughed and dismissed the resemblance as a coincidence.

As Sid left the Orlando terminal, he heard a scream. He turned and saw in horror that a large bus was veering up onto the sidewalk and heading straight for him. Then, suddenly, it stopped. Sid shivered in relief, amazed that it hadn't hit him.

He would have been more amazed had he been able to see the invisible figure of Michael, directing a mixed crew of demons and angels working together in concert for the first time since the Fall. They had stopped the bus and saved Sid's life. They were determined to keep Sid out of Heaven and out of Hell, even if it meant he would live to be a thousand. And he did.

Fundamentalist Christianity teaches that we live in the End Times – and have for two thousand years. A hundred generations have been born in the meanwhile, yet apocalyptic prophecies are as still prevalent today.

But what, Patrick Evans asks, if God is nothing like the doomsayers imagine? What if the true God is a deity Who can change longstanding positions on a whim? What if the true God embraces the sexual and excoriates war? In short, what if the image of God, as an old man with a white beard is absolutely, completely, utterly wrong?

MOUTH OF SATAN

PATRICK EVANS

Edith was an only child whose mother died giving birth to her at home. Pastor Morris, Edith's father, decreed that no child of God should be born in a hospital that treated homosexuals with AIDS. God's judgements were not to be defied, and every hospital in the city was rotting to its foundations with this sin.

Morris led a small Christian sect in Toronto which forbade girls to go to school. It was a sin to teach a female to read. Literacy leads to ideas and ideas threaten a woman's already paltry resistance to the Mouth of Satan between her legs. Bad enough females incited men to frenzies of lust with their undulating walk and fluttering lashes. Any emancipation of women's filthy desires would cause the flames of Hell to blast the surface of this world as in the world below.

And Pastor Morris knew Hell. As a child, Edith watched the Devil torment her father, spin a cyclone of rage through his body, slather the stink of gin on his tongue, and order him to her bed. She cried for him on those nights. She cried for herself, too. Surely she was damned for having had the Devil enter her? And she was doubly damned because when Morris showered her with fists that made the bed legs screech across the floor, a small, stricken part of Edith welcomed it. Morris was burdened with the moral well-being of his flock and therefore righteously stern, condemnatory, and remote. So remote. Edith was at home alone all day, year after year.

She had longed for a loving parent's touch. She had prayed to God for it, but received the Devil's touch instead.

As she well deserved. How dare she pray for her father's love when Christ's love alone should have sufficed?

But Jesus's mercy knows no bounds. Officially, Pastor Morris died of alcohol poisoning, but Edith knew that Jesus had thwarted Satan by stealing Morris away to Heaven where he'd be safe at last. His death coincided with Edith's first period and Jesus, in a second act of grace, rescued her from damnation by forever silencing her Mouth of Satan. He struck it dead.

At thirty, Edith was a tiny, birdlike woman with pinched features, thin suspicious brown eyes, and thin brown hair twisted in a penitentially tight bun. Her shoulders, knees and toes all rolled inward whether she sat or walked, as if to squeeze shut her body from the eyes of Satan and any who lust on his behalf. She dreaded the time that inevitably came, when she was pressured by the congregation matriarchs to marry and bear children, as was a woman's duty. At least she found a tolerable husband in Tony Peterson, who agreed with her that the sexual act was disgusting to God for any purpose but procreation – and even then any accidental pleasure in it made Jesus weep in equal measure. Edith didn't love Tony but she believed he was a virtuous man because it took him forever to produce an erection for the filthy act, yet he gave her three beautiful sons.

She had no idea that for years he was visiting public washrooms, damning himself in squalid acts with other men, until one night he told her everything and announced he was leaving her for a man named Marco, who was what's known as a 'personal trainer.' Edith was surprised a forked tongue didn't fall out of his mouth when he said, "Marco has shown me that sex is a celebration of God's love."

The shock threw Edith into a deep depression. She was nursed back to health by the ministrations and prayers of the women of the congregation. One woman, Ashley Hennessy – whose imposing size and stern reticence had always frightened Edith, always reminded her of her father – sat for hours at her bedside, as patient and gentle as Christ himself.

And when Edith finally got out of bed she wasn't just well; she was born anew, a living torch carrying the raging, devouring flame of the Holy Spirit. She had a Calling: It be the Lord's will that copulation is for procreation alone and any other urges are the assaults of Satan. Edith resolved to build a fortress where the truly faithful could defend themselves from the barrage of filth of this world, a fortress within which intercourse was strictly regulated to ensure procreation without pleasure, where the energies of the flock were liberated from sex for the proper worship and contemplation of the greatness of the Lord Almighty.

She would call it Purity, and establish it for all who wished to be saved, but especially for her sons – Michael, twelve, Matthew, eleven, and Jude, ten – whom the Devil would soon torment with longings of the flesh. There was no time to lose.

And no sooner did Edith conceive of this fortress than the Lord sent her an ally: Ashley Hennessy.

Ashley's body was as open as Edith's was closed. She was tall and broad-shouldered, strong-jawed, and had eyes so wide and blue it was as if the brightest Prairie skies rolled through them. She was a farmer and every inch of her conveyed a coarse vigor and confidence. Her prematurely gray hair was shorn to half an inch. She had no time for primping and preening.

Three months after Edith received her Calling, Ashley's husband Buzz died of a heart attack. Ashley, whom God in His wisdom had fashioned as a woman, alone owned the farm now, as provided for in Numbers 36:1-10. At the repast after the funeral, Edith stalked her, predatorily waiting for a moment alone with her.

"I did my duty by him," Ashley told Edith with a grim shrug. "When we learned we were never going to have children I told him to keep to his side of the bed and he pursued his debaucheries elsewhere. He died in a motel dressed as a blowfish. I don't know what it means and I don't care to."

A blowfish? Ashley's unblinking candor left Edith speechless. After stammering a bit she finally said, "We must grieve, then, for a soul gone astray."

"God help me, I'm not grieving. I'm finally free. No man will ever share my bed again."

"God loves you for your chastity," Edith said. "And I find you inspirational." She was unaware how calculating she looked just then, with her purposeful smile and a single eyebrow raised. "You inspire me on my mission."

"Mission?"

Edith described Purity to her.

"Where will you build?" Ashley said.

Edith shook her head. "I don't know. I just don't know. Somewhere far, far away from this city's filth."

"You got money to buy?"

"Money? Oh." Edith acted as if this was the first time it occurred to her. "Well, no. Oh, it's typical of me. I get these highfalutin' ideas, but with no head for business." She sighed despondently. "I can only pray for the Lord to show me the way."

Ashley's nodded, regarded her skeptically, and then said very simply, "We'll use my farm. I got no better use for it than giving it to the Lord. But I warn you, it's only thirty miles from the city."

"That's far enough!" Edith said, clapping her hands together in delight.

But Lord, Ashley. Didn't Ashley have eyes as blue as the Lamb of God Himself?

Edith was suddenly ashamed, as if a pair of mighty hands were squeezing her heart.

"Ashley. I'd be a sinner if I didn't confess—"

"You were angling for the farm all along?" Ashley chuckled. "Edith, I'd be a dummy if I hadn't known it."

Purity was a wheat farm with plenty of spare acreage for the community, which was culled from the Toronto congregation after a predictably rancorous schism, and a North American tour of fundamentalist churches undertaken by Edith and Ashley in Ashley's old Honda.

Within a few months, the men had erected a simple wooden chapel that leaked when it rained and two large dormitories, one for men, one for women, each with their own sleeping quarters and dining halls. Apart from random flashlight checks by Edith and Ashley during the night, the women were unsupervised. Really, what could a group of women get up to when they're cut off from males? What mattered was that their windows were painted shut and the door was locked at night, unsealed only by Edith and Ashley's keys or a fire alarm.

But because male flesh is known to run riot, cameras were taped the men's quarters, round the clock, showers included. Young Jude – whose whose adorable toddler's lisp troubled Edith by persisting into his adolesencce – volunteered for the task of scanning the tapes daily for signs of Sodomite activity.

As leaders of the congregation, Edith and Ashley knew their authority would be enhanced if they lived apart from it, and so they slept in twin beds in the master bedroom of the tiny old farmhouse Ashley had shared with Buzz. The only other bedroom in this house was where the married couples had their scheduled procreative sex – fifteen minutes during which Edith or Ashley stood outside the door with a stopwatch. They didn't want to end up like the Shakers, after all. Except for a mournful portrait of Christ, the room was unadorned, with a lumpy mattress and sagging bedsprings that ensured the lovers' next-day impression of the Necessary Evil would be sore backs.

From the start, Edith's boys read at the services. Edith sat with Ashley in the first pew, and the sight of them as the years wore on, taking more and more of a leadership role at Purity, filled her with pride. This happened often and every time it did, Edith caught herself, horror-struck. As always, whatever felt good to Edith almost immediately began to reek of sin. Wasn't pride was the first and foremost of the seven deadly sins? Didn't pride goeth before destruction? Merciful Jesus, was this contamination of Edith's own soul virulent enough to infect the objects of her pride, her boys? Michael was handsome and too confident by far, the cock-of-the-walk, turning the heads of all the young

121

women on their side of the chapel. Matthew was always so withdrawn, unreadable, never a smile or a scowl, his face just dead. And Jude, though full of cheerful devotion to Christ, was forbidden to review the men's quarters tapes after Edith discovered he was locking the door of the security booth while he worked.

When crises occurred, like young Susan and Malcolm running away, Edith would crumble with a sense of failure. Ashley's quiet, common-sense words of comfort would restore her again. Though the blurring of the sexes was perverse and sinful to Edith, she nonetheless adored Ashley's quiet confidence, so masculine and self-assured. For all Edith fretted and suffered every day of her life, in that little farm house she had found in Ashley the companionship and protection she had longed for since childhood.

For ten good years, Purity thwarted Satan.

And then Satan contrived to destroy it.

As the President of the General Assembly of the United Nations opened the 69th session in its New York headquarters, a striking little woman materialized beside him on the podium. She lightly touched his arm. He shivered, his face suddenly drained of blood, and stepped aside.

Even with heels on She was so short. She had to tug the podium microphone down to her mouth. The entire Assembly winced in pain as feedback shrieked through the speaker system. "Sorry about that," She said, wincing too. And then, recovering herself with a huge smile, She said, "Good morning, ladies and gentlemen." Her words were magically heard in the native tongue of everyone in the room. "I'd like to introduce myself if I may. I'm God."

She looked to be in Her late twenties. Her skin was a deep, impenetrable black, smooth as polished metal, and reflected knife-like shards of light with every movement. She had incredibly thick lips painted with a shining purple lipstick. Her blue eyes were also heavily made up, a gaudy gradation of baby blue and purple powders extending from Her eyelids to Her razor-thin fashion-model eyebrows. Her black hair was cropped to the skull and Her forehead so high that when She reared Her head with a posture both regal and seductive, She appeared to be altogether bald.

She was under five feet tall but compensated with six-inch high heels. She wore a tight black skirt and a trim black blazer with the lowest button done up. Her naked breasts were so large they forced back the blazer's lapels, spilling out for all to see, and tugging at the single done-up button below hard enough to tilt it slightly on its side.

A closed circuit TV recorded the meeting. God channeled the signal through every form of communication in the world. What was shut off She turned on – TVs, computers, mobile phones, radios. She appeared on e-books, interrupted films at the cinema. In primitive cultures, the footage ran on the surface of lakes and ponds. The Amish saw Her in their windows. An old lady with no television watched Her in the shine of her microwave door.

"My sudden appearance will be jarring for people of all faiths," God said, "especially since none of you got Me quite right. Now given the extraordinary claim I've just made, I think you'll agree our first order of business should be proof of My Divinity. I warn you, something very unsettling is about to happen, but please rest assured you're all perfectly safe."

The domed General Assembly building groaned. And then

the entire structure – floor, ceiling, pillars, walls, pipes, ducts – silently split apart and flew into the sky, dragging a fat tail of dust. The people who had been on the various floors of the building, the Assembly in its rows of crescent-shaped tables and God at the podium, all floated in mid-air. They watched as the pieces of the building crashed together above them: concrete, brick and plaster, exploding into dusty clouds, which then imploded as if inhaled by some giant lungs; the steel framework broke down to its individual girders, each of which folded in on itself again and again; all of it rolled furiously into a smaller and smaller ball until the entire building was compacted into a tiny, gold cylindrical object, which fell from the sky into the hand of God.

It was a lipstick. She smiled, turned the cylinder, and rolled a fresh layer of purple over Her lips.

Everyone was screaming.

God held the lipstick in the palm of Her hand. It turned to dust. She blew the dust over the podium and an instant later, the building was fully restored.

"I could exert a calming influence," She said softly, "but I think you're more than entitled to your feelings right now."

An older man wearing a turban stood up and though his hands trembled, he spoke without any trace of fear in his voice. "What manner of God are you?"

"Good question, Sanjit. Is it okay if I call you Sanjit?" she said. "I'm what you'd call a Demiurge. The Prime Mover. I created the 'stuff' of the universe, set it in motion, and let it do its thing. By 'stuff' I mean energy and the sub-atomic particles that eventually formed atoms and elements and all that chemistry and physics jazz. But yeah, the Big Bang – that was me."

"And are You the only god?" he said.

"In this infinity, yes."

"There is more than one infinity?"

"Oh, yes. Infinitely more."

"But an infinity by definition extends forever. Where are these other infinities?"

"Picture a parking lot, Sanjit. Each infinity takes up one parking space in the lot. And the lot itself is infinite."

"Your metaphor fails you, my dear," he said smugly. It was clear by the increasingly scornful tone of his voice that he was trying to expose Her as a fraud, despite the miracle he'd just witnessed. "A parking space is finite. How can it accommodate an infinity?"

She smiled softly. "It ain't easy. You gotta back the car in real, real slow."

A woman stood up and asked in German. "Why are You here? Why now?"

"Another good question. I've had a lot of commitments the last fourteen billion years. But I was at a dinner party the other night and someone started making cracks about this one infinity with this really nasty race, and the Holocaust was specifically mentioned. We were all shaking our heads at how awful this place was, until I figured out we were talking about one of My universes. So I made some inquiries, and it turns out you motherfuckers have been pulling shit like the Holocaust ever since you came down from the trees." She shook Her head. "I was mortified. And disgusted. I love you all, but 'motherfuckers' pretty much says it. I'm here to get you back on track."

"You have dinner parties?" the woman said.

"I'm speaking metaphorically about non-anthropomorphic numinous phenomena beyond human language or comprehension. But yeah, dinner parties."

Her smile was playful.

"Look, folks, I understand you need time to absorb all this.

125

You'll all decide I'm an intolerable threat. You'll deny My Incarnation and call me the Antichrist, or Iblis, or Rahu, or Mara, or a space invader, or some horny teenager's basement science experiment gone awry. Whatever your different cultures need me to be, so long as I'm not God. You'll all pull together to destroy Me. You'll have America's entire arsenal on your side – which is great because they have the best shit for blowing up obnoxious divine upstarts with slutty tits. So let's get all that out of the way. Why don't you kill Me on, say, May 15? Now, a lot of you will decide this is the big apocalyptic battle your faith predicts, and you're perfectly entitled to believe that. But I'll pick My own battlefield if you don't mind, and I'd like to go with the Arabian desert. You choose the exact spot. Just paint a big target in the sand and I'll be on it."

And then She vanished.

At Purity Edith was summoned to the security booth. Ashley and Michael sat watching the monitor, both white as a shroud. The scene at the United Nations was playing on the digital cartridge of the men's showers in an endless loop. Edith was furious. "It's a trick," she said, yanking the cartridge out of the drive. The monitor, with no feed from the outside world, continued to play the scene.

They watched it three times. Edith could see how desperately Ashley wanted to be strong for her every time they watched the General Assembly pull apart. But on the third viewing Ashley looked up at her and started to shake violently.

"I ... I don't understand ... who ... who ..." Ashley stammered.

"Shh," Edith said. For once, she would be the strong one.

"Who that woman is!"

"That's no woman. That's the Antichrist. And you know who smites the Antichrist. You heard it declare war. The Battle of Armageddon. These are End Times."

Michael buried his face in his hands.

"God help us," Ashley said.

Edith's face was red with anger. "You two! Where is your joy? Christ is coming! Of all generations, we are blessed to witness the fruition of God's great plan! Think of the happiness of this day!"

"It's just …" The tremendous weight of terror in Ashley's voice was making it fold in on itself until she was almost inaudible. Edith wasn't sure, but it sounded as if Ashley said, "I was already happy."

And before she could rout it a sinful thought stole across Edith's mind: I was happy too. Edith felt her legs turn to rubber. This thought frightened her in ways she couldn't bear to understand. Rather than try, she thought instead about the painted whore who called herself God, and was surprised to find herself screaming in terror.

On May 15th a large round wooden platform painted like an archery target waited in the sand of the Arabian desert.

In Her heels and business suit, God appeared in the center of the target. Satellite cameras broadcasted the event to the entire world.

She looked at the sky and down came the laser-armed satellites, and then the missiles, which were en route, including one nuke, all in pieces, clattering to the desert floor like a rain of cutlery. She nodded slightly and the thousands of tanks and troops who waited in reserve sixty miles away materialized in front of Her. Their tanks and guns fell to pieces.

Miles behind the terrified soldiers came a deafening, crashing sound. They turned to see five four-hundred foot tsunami waves, higher than any wave ever measured, crashing into one another. Spray from the explosion hit the soldiers like a thousand tiny insect stings. The waters buckled and roiled and finally settled across the desert in a brand new sea, its shoreline establishing itself in a softly rolling foam less than a mile from where the soldiers stood.

Then, directly beneath the soldiers' feet, grass and flowers grew. With the speed of a trail of gasoline burning, the vegetation spread all around them, travelling back to the seashore and ahead, past God on Her platform, miles away to the horizon.

"The lawn and flowers are really just to make the point that this land is fertile again," God said. "You'll need it for the population explosion coming up." She walked to the edge of the giant wooden target and reached down to pick a dahlia. "You all ready now for My big Revelation?"

The only response was the hornet-buzz of a dry desert wind that hadn't yet realized its desert was gone.

"Okay, hear this. I want you all to love each other. Not in a hippie-dippy love-thy-neighbor way, though that would be nice." She smiled and ran her fingers over her breasts. "I mean sexual love. I mean go forth and fuck your brains out. I'm talking hot monogamy. Rampant promiscuity. First-date sex. Man-on-man action. Lesbian lick-fest. Swingin' seniors' hot-tub orgies. Leather. Rubber. Old men dressed as high-school cheerleaders. If it gets you hot, do it.

"Now, what about AIDS and other diseases? Unwanted pregnancies? Dick chafing? Remember, I'm a demiurge –I created the materials of the universe, gave 'em a good stir, and took off to let them form their own relationships. There isn't, and never was, any determinism, so your varying notions of sexual morality throughout the millennia have all been valiant improvisations on the fly, to prevent everything from unwanted children to syphilis and cold sores. You did your best, even where repression destroyed lives. But as of today, all that stuff is gone. I'm making this easy for you. No more HIV. No more cold sores. No more penicillin or morning after pills. If you want a baby, both of you will it. Otherwise, girls, just enjoy that cock for its own sake.

"But no non-consensual sex. Rapists be warned. It's gonna fall off. I'm not talking metaphorically. I'm talking 'plop,' and, 'Oh my God, my dick fell off, put it on ice, maybe the hospital can reattach it.' I'll tell you now, the hospital can't. Don't anyone test me on this. Ladies, this includes you too. Give it a couple of weeks and I guarantee you'll be able to see pics online of what a vagina looks like when it falls out."

God put her finger to her lips and thought for a moment. "Hmm. I covered the old guys dressed as cheerleaders. What did I miss? Oh, right. Leave kids and animals out of it. They can't give informed consent, so don't even try it. That goes back to my 'plop' warning."

She tugged her blazer to straighten it. "Right. World leaders – if you try to rebuild all these weapons when you could be using those assembly lines for radical experiments in group sodomy, they're just gonna fall apart again. Quit being such assholes."

She vanished.

In the weeks that followed God appeared in multiple places at once. She'd be on a Russian talk show elaborating on Her edict: "Procreation isn't for ensuring the survival of a species. It's for ensuring the survival of sex via future generations. Sex is primary. It generates essential energies." At the same time, She'd be on an American talk show explaining why Her outfit stays the same, but She never wears the same shoes twice: "I have so many shoes, and you kinda feel sorry for them, sitting around unworn." And at the same time She was in five homes around the world snapping in half, with just a glance, the legs of fathers and brothers moving in for the honor killing of a woman who had asserted her sexual independence.

In all religions were instances where those who adhered to the old faith waged war against those who embraced the new God. She appeared at every violent skirmish, parting the factions, disintegrating their weapons, and with a wave of her hand commanded all of the combatants to piss and shit themselves.

"Next time you decide to aim a weapon at your fellow man, get yourself a big ol' diaper first."

The only deaths she didn't prevent were the suicides, and there were thousands worldwide among the faithful who could not endure the loss of their traditional deity. God told *The Washington Post,* "Suicide is a choice. It's a tragic choice. But it's the right of those who are unable to accept My divinity, or even just ignore it and just get on with starting their breakfast."

And many worldwide couldn't accept it. Most were outraged at the loss of their traditional god. Many were furious at the effrontery of a woman, or a shameless woman, or a black woman claiming to be the Highest Power. One newspaper editorialized that God would certainly be taller, and another, with the gravity of the greatest theologians, argued that the stress Her breasts were placing on that bottom button of Her blazer was proof She was a fake: a true deity would have a better tailor.

The conflict at Purity mirrored the worldwide conflict. At first the community was defiant, praying louder and longer, beseeching the Lord to crush the Painted Whore. But even when there was still hope that Christ would appear to smite this Outrage, Edith felt like a marked woman. Was the congregation whispering about her in the dining hall with sidelong glances? Was she a fool to have built a church so soon before the Apocalypse, a church that tolerated copulation to produce children who would never be born?

And then, after the Battle of Armageddon, Purity splintered. Among its most fanatical personalities, half insisted that Jesus refused to appear at the battle because the international attack force was contaminated by heathens. The other half was so impressed by the new God's power that they left in an ecstatic fever to help build new temples, which were rising everywhere. Some at Purity were thrilled to be freed from their sexual restraints. Young lovers made a run for it through the wheat fields.

In some cases it was the parents who never became grandparents who bolted, leaving behind their defiantly chaste grown children to pray for their souls.

Michael ran off with Diane, Purity's organist, a woman of forty.

Matthew just disappeared. No note. As inscrutable as always, he left in the night at the behest of whatever unknown desires or darkness motivated him.

Jude stayed, conducting the church services, trying with all the charisma of his starry personality to inspire a congregation that sat haunted in desolate pews where the hips of the faithful were once practically fused together.

Neither Edith nor Ashley appeared in the chapel anymore.

Edith had responded to the Battle of Armageddon and the abandonment of her sons by falling into another severe depression. The Painted Whore's decree of sexual liberty had voided her life's mission and, after an initial mania of defiant rage, she broke. She couldn't get out of bed or eat. Her tiny body shrank from 110 pounds to 70.

Ashley never left Edith's side, holding her hand and desperately visualizing the abundant strength of her body flowing into Edith's dwindling frame. She fed her soups, each spoonful a long and bitter negotiation.

Christ, Satan, the Painted Whore – damn all these inflated monsters treating the world as a plaything, Ashley thought. If Christ wept at Ashley's blasphemy, then let him bloody well appear and restore the woman she loved.

And then one night God came to Purity.

The clacking of Her heels on the brick of the courtyard outside the chapel during the evening service announced Her presence. Jude, who had never heard high heels inside the compound before, instinctively knew to whom they belonged and hurried down from the pulpit. Ashley, at Edith's bedside, recognized them too and quietly slipped away as Edith slept. She met her outside the chapel with Jude and the awed remains of the congregation.

"I'm sorry it took Me so long to visit," God said. Wispy clouds skittered across a full moon. She glimmered in the changing light like a diamond turning in a jeweler's hands. "Jude, when you question My divinity you focus on My shoes. You think I make some hideous choices that a true God wouldn't be caught dead in."

He did. He slipped his hands into his pockets and looked down. He was shaking.

She came forward and placed her hand on his arm.

"You're right. Those faux alligator skin open-toes I had on

last week? No wonder you're still preaching from the Bible."

Sheepishly, he glanced at her face.

"But my touch has dispelled your doubts, hasn't it? You know I am who I say I am. Now, Jude. No disrespect to your mother, sweetie. But she's a miserable old hag determined to remake the world in her own bitter and repressed image. And it's because her father was a monster who neglected, beat, and raped her as a child."

Jude gasped.

"But Jude, those are your mother's scars. You mustn't wear them. Get the fuck out of here and live in truth. Find your dad in Toronto. His greatest shame is that he abandoned you boys. He loves you, and he and his partner, Marco, can help you."

Ashley wanted to intervene to protect Edith's interests. But she was speechless. Her jaw moved up and down as she mouthed in silent horror the words *neglected, beaten, raped.*

"Leave him be," came a fierce but quavering voice.

Edith's emaciated form approached in the dark.

Ashley hurried over to take her arm. "You were asleep. I didn't want you to—"

"To what?" Edith snapped. "Defend my own home against the Devil?"

"Ashley intended to defend it for you," God said. "She'd do anything for you."

Edith stopped within a hand's span of God. "In the name of Christ, begone from this sacred ground!"

"Edith, there's a psychological phenomenon called cognitive dissonance," God said. "Sometimes when presented with overwhelming evidence that long-held beliefs are incorrect, a person will hold on to those old beliefs harder than ever. It's very human. And in your case, it's making you sick. Your body is rebelling against the fixity of your mind."

"Devil's rhetoric," Edith said with a wild, ferocious smile. "Oh, she's a master of it! Is it because I'm a woman that you're using these five-dollar words? Cognitive dissonance. Fixity! Remind me, what were your words in the desert? Oh, yes. You said, 'I covered the guys dressed as cheerleaders. What did I miss? Oh – of course. Leave animals and kids out of it too.' I watched you and I wondered, does the one true God really have such a disorganized mind?"

"You already know the answer to that."

"Oh, I do! I recognize all your ways! The manipulative co-quette. You talk to women as equals. But when your audience includes men, from soldiers to world leaders, like all whores you know that acting scatterbrained and coy gets you what you want."

"Like when you got Ashley to offer her farm for Purity."

Edith staggered back. Her chest heaved with a wave of rage and shame.

God smiled. "Edith, you're right. I am a manipulative whore in this persona. And that's what you need to understand. What you're seeing is a persona, not My true face. It's a manipulation, but for a good cause."

Bolstered by Edith's courage, Ashley chimed in. "So you're not a bimbo. But we're supposed to believe you could create the universe but not foresee the Holocaust?"

"Absolutely. See, I have a bunch of different aspects. The 'Me' you're talking to is Omnipotence. Another aspect is Omnisci-ence. He saw what was coming, but I chose not to. Our separa-tion created a gap that gave you free will. Not Our best decision, depending on who you ask. Some of you kill. And some, like you, Edith, destroy yourselves. But given your history, you deserve a real shot at happiness. A choice. This will help."

She smiled, and Edith was restored to her former, healthy

weight.

Edith recoiled as if she'd just been splashed by paint. Then she lurched forward and slapped God's cheek. "Devil!"

God rubbed her cheek in amusement. "What's so cool about you, Edith, is you've got the stones to bitch-slap God."

Ashley, pulling Edith back, started to cry. "Thank you," she whispered to God.

Edith turned to Ashley furiously. The black fire in her eyes said it all.

"I don't care if she's the Devil," Ashley wept. "She gave you back to me!"

Edith turned back to God. "Hear me, Satan—"

"No, you hear Me," God said. "You've touched Me, and now you know what I am. So cut the denial. You've been in a lesbian relationship for ten years now, and you never once told your soul mate you love her. I'm dying to see you two bump uglies, but the very least you can do is acknowledge your life would be empty without Ashley."

"Damn you and your filth!"

"Edith, the only person in this world who will never desert you is Ashley."

"Jude has stood by me!"

"Jude's leaving," God said.

Edith and Ashley and the others in the congregation looked to Jude. Trembling, but with a firm jaw, he nodded.

And when they looked back to God, She was gone.

A day later only Edith and Ashley remained at Purity.

The two women sat in silence on the couch in the living room of their little house. Though it was June, they built a fire in the hearth. The firelight and crackling logs comforted them.

Finally, Edith pulled a balled-up piece of plastic wrap from her pocket. "Ashley. I have something." She carefully smoothed the wrap over the coffee table. Two tiny pink pills sat in the center.

"Oh, Edith," Ashley said. "That's not – where did you get that?"

"Those who have stayed true to Christ are collaborating. We're rising above our differences to share ... options."

Ashley's breath quickened. "I'm not taking that. You're giving me cyanide, Edith?" Tears formed in her eyes. "You know it's a sin to ..."

"It is the lesser sin," Edith interrupted. "The greater sin is to abide in a world corrupted by that creature. Ashley, wake up! Hell has burst its gates and consumed this world! The only path out of these flames is the one leading directly to Jesus Christ!"

Ashley stood up anxiously. Her shin smacked the edge of the coffee table as she moved around to the hearth. She stared at the fire for a moment and then turned around, hissing her words. "Before you lived here, that coffee table was always three feet from the couch. Look at me, Edith! I'm built like brick shit house! You think I can just tiptoe past that thing like a fucking ballerina? I hit my shin every day, I push the damn table out, and when I'm not around you pull it right back in where you want it! Ten years, Edith!"

Edith shrugged. "We can push it back," she said innocently. Then she mumbled, "God knows how I'll reach my tea."

Ashley stomped forward. "Oh, I could strangle you, sometimes, Edith. But you're not killing either of us tonight. I don't give a damn about religion anymore. I don't care who's the real god. All I know is that woman was right about us. I've loved you for ten years and you've loved me. To Hell with the rest of it!"

Edith stood up, furious. She walked cleanly around the coffee table over to Ashley, stared her down for a moment, and said, "She's possessed you!"

"Bullshit! We built a home and a life together, and the one thing, the one thing, Edith, we've never done, is touch each other and say, 'I love you.'"

Turning away, Edith said, "I'm praying for you."

Ashley caught her arm and spun her around. "Admit it!" She tried to wrap her arms around Edith, who fought back, pushing and squirming. "Admit it!"

"Don't you touch me."

"Admit it!"

"Don't."

"Admit it!"

Edith screamed.

Neglected. Beaten. Raped.

Ashley let go of Edith and backed away to the fireplace with a wail of grief, and started crying heavily.

Edith struggled to draw breath. Ashley was always so stolid she suffered just showing enthusiasm for a birthday cake. It was unbearable to see her cry. Edith staggered forward with the uncertain gait of a drunk, touched Ashley very tentatively on her collarbone, and then threw her arms around her. The women stood holding each other by the flames, both crying for a very long time.

"I love you, Ashley," Edith finally whispered. "God save me."

"I love you too," Ashley said, squeezing the breath out of her. "My Edith."

When Ashley woke in the morning Edith's bed was already

made. The uncompromisingly smooth bedspread, the impossibly tight corners, the same as always – but somehow, today, Ashley recognized it as a grim omen. Horror and grief forced her eyes shut and made her head swim for a moment. Then she ran downstairs.

Of course. There was Edith. Dead on the couch.

Both pills gone.

Edith had taken one pill to silence forever her Mouth of Satan, resurrected the night before, and spewing the filth her father had warned her against.

She took the other pill so the woman she loved might live.

It's unfathomable how much evil has been done in the name of God. Then again, if God exists, it's also worth asking how much evil He's done independently of his sales reps.

If you could kill God, would you? David J. Fielding's narrator wouldn't even hesitate – even if the result of an end to evil was just another form of the absence of good.

TIME STOPS FOR NO MAN

DAVID J. FIELDING

If you want a definitive answer, then yes there is a God ... or was, I should say.

It took a lot of work, but I finally found the old bastard. And then I killed him.

So you can blame me for the way things are – or praise me, either way I don't give a good goddamn.

I follow pretty much the same routine these days, but you are probably familiar. If you are anything like me and chances are pretty good that you are, then you have a routine too. It may not be anything like my routine; in fact it probably is totally and completely different. But if I tell you mine, you'll probably recognize a pattern.

I get up about the same time every day, maybe a little before or maybe a little bit after seven.

A.M.

The morning.

I wake up but I don't open my eyes right away. I savor the rapidly fading feeling of sleep, of the dreams that dissolve and fade like fog. Then I roll over to my right and open my eyes, to see the same thing I see every morning. Daylight streaming through my penthouse window.

You don't live in a penthouse? OK. To each his own I guess. There's plenty around – just take your pick.

I then swing my feet over the edge of the soft, clean sheets and dig my toes into the deep pile carpet, kneading the soft fabric. It feels fantastic. I stare out the window at the sunlight that is bouncing off the glass buildings and skyscrapers. Call me old-fashioned but I love living in the city. Of course, the buzz and energy isn't what it used to be.

I lever myself up off the bed and pad my way over to the dresser. I slip into my workout clothes, grab my keys (out of habit more than anything else) and step out of the apartment and take a short walk to the elevators. Some days I choose the left one, sometimes the right. I used to try to make it a different choice each day, but decided in the end it really didn't matter.

I get in the elevator and punch the button for the pool level on the third floor. A number of apartment complexes I looked at had their athletic facilities on different floors. This building has a running track on the roof for example. But I don't use it.

I step off the elevator and enter the gym area – pretty standard: weights, mirrors, treadmills, the works. I go through my workout, finishing with a five-mile run on the treadmill. The treads line the windows looking out over the street and I watch as the rest of the city's inhabitants go about their business.

I would say their routines, but I've noticed that a lot of the routines consist mainly of standing around or sitting in the street with their heads in their hands.

After my workout I take a shower. The water is always hot; almost scalding. It feels wonderful.

After the shower I grab my breakfast from the fridge: fresh fruit, juice and a small bowl of oatmeal. It's the same every morning but I don't get tired of it.

It was there waiting for me when I took over the apartment and I just never thought about much about it. Don't really see the point, considering.

Then I grab my journal and begin writing it all down.

Again.

From the beginning.

I spend the day writing, grabbing lunch if I feel like it and then I spend the evening watching the sun go down over the bay. I love to watch the light sparkle off the water. Then I go to bed. And I sleep. Sometimes I dream … or I think I dream. I can't be sure because even dreaming seems routine. Repetitious.

And I get up the next day and do it all over again.

I wake up, I work out, I eat breakfast and I write.

It's my penance you can say. Not that it will change anything and not that anybody will ever read what I write, considering it gets erased or reset or whatever you want to call it.

It's annoying but you get used to it. Well, some of us do.

There's a window of opportunity that some have discovered that allows them to escape the whole round-and-round of what existence has become. I found it a long time ago, and seeing as how I'm the one responsible for how things are, I don't really feel it would be right of me to take advantage of it. Guilt you say? Hardly. I like the way things are. Or I should say the way things aren't. Because things really aren't anything. They are the same. Day in and day out. All over the world.

I'm used to it.

Hell, I was used to it long before I pulled the trigger.

Here, let me explain it a bit better …

About ten years ago, or so it seems, I found myself in a pretty ugly set of circumstances. Life had done me dirty you could say, and I was pretty darn close to putting a gun in my mouth. I had nothing, no one on my side and no prospects of putting things to rights.

I'm not gonna go into details, you've heard 'em all before anyway: fired from a job, a wife who walked out, creditors took all my money. Didn't have nothing but the clothes on my back and twenty something bucks to my name. And nothing I tried, nothing I did could change it. I was stuck, literally – couldn't go forward, couldn't go back.

So there I was, on the street. And after nearly three years of this, my mind was numb, I had no new ideas of what to do or where to begin.

How did I get that low? How does anybody? A bad choice here, a stupid mistake there, a run of bad luck. What does it matter? What matters was I was there, in that place and on that street corner.

But right then, at that very moment, that's when I found the way to fix everything.

I was in the 'Burgh at the time – drifted there and just ended up staying, tired of floating from place to place I guess. Anyway, I was standing on the corner of Fifth and Forbes down from Mellon Institute, cardboard sign in one hand, begging for change. And that's when I heard him laughing.

This street corner is close to the college campus and, it being springtime, there were lots of students roaming about, some rushing to class, some heading to the shops and restaurants on Craig Street, others just out enjoying the sunshine.

I hated them all. Not really hated them, but hated that I was me, with my sad-sack life and they were them with their carefree lives.

And I heard that laugh. It was a rough and raucous laugh, a real belly laugh. Mean.

I looked around and didn't see anything at first. No one else seem to notice the sound and for a moment I thought I was going crazy, that it was all in my head.

Then I saw him.

He was standing across the street, by the bus stop, just behind the crowd waiting for the A1 making its way up the street. He was tall, a good six-foot-nine, grizzled, looked to be in his eighties if he was a day.

Pants too short, ugly green socks pulled up too high, worn vest, dirty shirt, long tattered tan coat. He had a shirt with frilly lace and a goddamn pocket watch, if you can believe that. Who the hell wears a pocket watch? His balding head was ringed with wild scraggly hair and his hawk nose supported those silly, out-of-date, purple hippie shades. He looked like some sort of circus act, wearing a costume – a carnival freak.

He was standing there laughing.

And pointy one bony finger right at me.

I looked about stupidly, as though there were anyone else he could be pointing at. That made him laugh harder.

And then I heard him, as though he were standing next to me, his voice right next to my ear.

"Time stops for no one, sonny – though I do slow down and taunt those I leave behind!"

And then he was laughing again and the crowd was piling onto the bus. I craned my neck, trying to keep him in my line of vision, but the people were packed on the bus and he was gone.

If he had even been there in the first place.

I thought I had finally gone and done it, slipped over the edge. I was one of those crazy people.

I retreated, finished begging for the day, and hoofed it back to my hiding spot off the street behind some of the shops. So far the regular cops and campus police hadn't been notified where I was and I'd been able to stay there for about a week. I got to my spot, curled up on the cardboard and shut my eyes, trying to tell myself I wasn't crazy, that what I had seen was just ... I don't know. A fluke, a dizzy spell ... something ...

I actually fell asleep.

I woke up with a start. The scene replaying itself in my dreams. And I knew, without a doubt who he was.

He was Time. Somehow, some way, he was Time – the actual, physical manifestation of Time. And by that I mean he was God.

Because what is God if not Time?

God is love you say? Bullshit. Love is fickle and love dies; love is not eternal.

Time is unending. It moves on, uncaring, unfeeling. It marches eternally onward. Inexorable.

Time is the one thing we cannot deny.

Maybe Tide stops for no man, as the saying goes, but Time did for me. I was stuck. And I guess that was what he found so funny.

So I knew what I had to do.

I snuck into the Carnegie Library and I looked it up, all the stuff that had been written about Time. What it was (well, theories about what it was), how it worked, the whole nine yards. And then I started looking for anything I could find about people who had claimed to see Time. I logged onto one of the computers in the library and surfed the web for hours.

I went back to that library day after day, for weeks. Sure I got escorted out quite a bit, and when they prevented me from getting in, I would find other libraries or campus computers I could use.

I hitched to DC, wandered in the Library of Congress, looked up all their resources. I found as many resources as I could, jotted it all down in a notebook I'd stolen out of some kid's backpack. Got escorted out of there, too.

And I researched everything I could about God. I read and listened and spoke to scholars and priests and holy men and holy women.

And I knew my instinct was correct. I knew that I had seen God, had seen Time on that corner that day.

You see, I had found out things. Weird things, and what I found out was that God, that Time, is really an asshole. And killing him was what really needed to happen. In the whole history of things, what had this being really done for me? For any of us?

He just keeps moving, changing, fucking everything up.

He deserved to be taken out.

So I dug deeper.

I read and reread everything and anything I could find about what it takes to challenge an omnipresent being.

I mean, how do you hunt a thing that knows you are hunting it? Turns out it's not as hard as you think.

Why?

Because he didn't care. He was oblivious to everything. He was just going about his routine.

So I tried to establish what the routine was. After a long hitch back to Chicago, I started back on the street corner. Then I moved to the bus stop. And I could feel that he'd been there. Even weeks after I'd seen him. The stop was different, more charged, something like that. There was something there, an energy, a feeling ... can't really explain it. But this feeling, this energy, it pointed me to the next spot. And that one pointed to the next and the next and the next and the next.

I tracked him.

For years.

And then, not too long ago – it's hard to tell now, considering there's no way to measure it – I found him.

He was walking down the street in Chicago. A real arrogant, lanky walk, hands in his pockets, a stupid grin on his face.

I followed him. He was just going about the streets, no aims, no goals.

I picked my moment and worked my way so that I was ahead of where he was walking.

And then I stepped out in front of him.

He stopped, that stupid grin on his face.

"I know you, sonny!" he said.

"Yeah," I said. "And I know you."

I fired the gun seven times into his chest.

He looked surprised. The sound was really loud on the street and for just a second, everything stopped. It's like everything wound down … like when a battery runs out of energy and the song you are listening to winds and grinds down to a halt? Like that. Everything stopped.

Time. Sight. Sound.

Everything.

And then, like a piece of music catching up to the right speed, things caught back up to real time. But only later would every-one realize that not everything went back to normal.

The old man look at the smoking holes in his chest, then at me, and his eyes rolled back in his head and he fell over. He was done.

People around us fled.

It was only later, much later, would we learn that Time had stopped.

And that's where we are, boys and girls, so you can thank me or hate me, I really don't care.

Now you are all like me.

Stuck. Not going forward, not going back.

There ain't no change, there ain't no death and there ain't nothing anybody can do about it.

There's just the endless routine: wake up, work out, have breakfast and writing. No war, no disease, no heartbreak, no joy, no sadness … no change.

You're welcome.

Many, not least of all Einstein, pondered the question, "If God created the universe, did He have a choice?" Could He have just let well enough alone and not set it all in motion?

Conversely, we could ask if God has a choice about ending the universe. Brian K. Lowe would like to understand that better. And now that we are all, at His behest, here, would He consult us before making the decision?

COMMITMENT

BRIAN K. LOWE

I found the Archangel Gabriel sitting on a bench in the park.

He was just resting there, his horn sitting in his lap as though he'd been playing for the quarters passers-by would drop in the overturned hat on the sidewalk at his feet. The nearest street lamp was burned out, but in the glow in the lamp down the path a ways, I could see that his coat was worn and his trousers were shiny at the knees.

He had the kind of dark skin that doesn't show wrinkles, making it impossible to tell how old he might be. But of course he wasn't just some old black musician, down on his luck and years removed from his days with Benny Goodman – he was the Archangel Gabriel, and he was sitting on my bench.

I lowered myself onto the wet wood next to him, my bones cracking and snapping like breakfast cereal. Nobody walked by for him to play for. It was long past midnight, still dark but much closer to dawn. Dew had started to settle on the ground and sleeping statues. But if he didn't mind the solitude and the wet bench, why then, I didn't either. At least those things I had been expecting. Gabriel didn't speak when I sat down, nor move nor raise his head either.

Even so late – or so early, depending on how you reckon time – I could hear the murmur of cars on the boulevard, out of sight behind the big old dying elm trees. A long time ago I stopped wondering why business kept people out at such hours, including me. It was our pact; I didn't ask them and they didn't ask me.

"You know who I am," he said at last. It was a question without a question mark. He knew I knew; he just needed me to know I could trust myself.

"Yes," I said, nodding a bit, though he hadn't looked at me. "When I was a boy, my mother was always looking for the Truth, even though she didn't have any idea where to find it. One Sunday she dragged me to a Baptist church downtown. We were the only white people there. Even the figures in the murals and paintings were African. I've never forgotten that. On the wall directly opposite our pew was a painting of Gabriel appearing before the Virgin Mary. He had your face."

His head was still back on the bench, watching Heaven.

"Do you believe it?"

"I'm sorry?"

"You know it, but do you believe it?"

I thought he must be playing with me. "Isn't that the same thing?"

"No." He wasn't arguing with me, more like resigned to letting me have my point of view. "Do you know why I'm here?" he asked abruptly.

"No," I admitted.

He opened his eyes and looked straight ahead. "It's time."

"Oh." There was a little flutter in my stomach – I would have thought it would be in my heart, but no matter. I pulled in a deep breath of cold morning, looked around at the elms that were going to outlast me after all, straightened my frayed cuffs, and looked at him. "All right then. Let's go."

Gabriel smiled sadly at the sky. "No, not for you, Arthur. For everything."

Well, that was unexpected. The flutter in my stomach went away, replaced by curiosity, and maybe a bit of excitement, the kind of guilty excitement you feel when you think maybe there's going to be a fight.

"Really?" I felt like a kid again, that Christmas when I saw a big present under the tree and it had my name on it.

Gabriel nodded at last. "Really."

"You don't look very happy about it." In the dark, I heard the material of his jacket move as he shrugged.

"It gets old after a while."

I frowned. "You've done this before?"

He sighed. "About a thousand times. Whenever it's necessary. It's not for the whole universe, just for you folks, but it happens to everyone eventually."

"Everyone? You mean …?"

"Yes," he said. My eyes grew wide. I looked up, as he was doing, but instead of heaven I saw the billions of other lives I'd always dreamed about, revolving around thousands of other suns. "It's a shame you never got to meet any of the others."

I was thrown back to earth. "Would it have helped?"

His voice was very soft. "No."

My dreams dashed, we fell into silence again. The street murmurs had grown almost imperceptibly louder, but not so much as to break the spell. The day was approaching.

I was fearful to rouse him, afraid to hasten whatever terrible calamity the rage of heaven might take, but his silence was an invitation, engraved on the air.

"So why me? Why my bench?"

He sighed with palpable relief. "Because I only carry the horn. I don't blow it. That has to be one of you. It's the last test of free will."

"But why me? I haven't been to church in years."

"But I believe you still have faith. As tattered and fragile as it is, you still believe."

That was news to me. "I'm afraid I stopped believing in anything besides this bench a long time ago." I thought about that big present, and the morning I unwrapped it to find it was only a much smaller toy my parents had stuffed in a big box to fool me. "I don't know if I believe in God any more. I used to, but now I'm just kind of an agnostic."

So why not just blow the horn? What difference will it make? a voice in my head taunted. But I had no answer.

Gabriel chuckled almost silently. "No you're not, Arthur. An agnostic is nothing but an atheist with a fear of commitment. Maybe you haven't been to church in seventeen years, but you're a good man; in many ways you're the most honest man on Earth. In the ways that count, Arthur," he said quickly, as if he knew my objection. "In the ways that only you and I can see. You never betrayed yourself. Besides," he added with more warmth, "you play." He indicated the trumpet in his lap. "Anybody could play it – but it sounds best when it's in the hands of a man who knows how. I think your world deserves that."

"What happens if I play it?"

"The world ends."

That was when I realized he was crazy. I don't know why I hadn't realized it before; maybe I wasn't cut out for these late nights any more. He wasn't an archangel any more than I was the reincarnation of Britain's legendary king. He thought I could play, and I hadn't played since the day I realized that no matter how long I practiced I'd never be in a real orchestra, never be anything more than third trumpet in a mediocre high school band. I'd had faith in that dream, knew if I worked hard enough I could make it someday – and it never happened. Just like I never became a great lawyer, never more than a one-man personal injury office. That was where my faith had gone. It had faded with my dreams.

And the last of all, held with white-knuckled intensity, had been the one dream I'd thought Life couldn't take away. After all, you can't really know if you were right about God until you're dead, and then it's a little late to worry about whether you were wrong. But I had been wrong, when I thought there was a dream, a hope, that Life couldn't extinguish. I had counted on logic to sustain hope, but I had not counted on how long a life can be, how many disappointments one can be asked to endure.

But here He was. Not God Himself, but as close as you could ask for. Or so said some out-of-work musician who couldn't afford a bed for the night.

"Arthur," Gabriel said with soft urgency, and I realized only then that I'd risen to my feet. "I picked you for this because you still aren't lost. You still want to believe. But if you walk away from me now, you won't have another chance. Someone else will blow it, someone who may not have your faith."

"What do you mean? What difference does it make? The world is going to end. You said so yourself." I was beginning to doubt myself. What was I doing, talking to some stranger in the park at five in the morning?

"It makes a great deal of difference, Arthur. It literally makes all the difference in the world. If you blow the horn out of faith, faith that something more awaits, something that you cannot see, then something better will come. But if he who blows the horn does it simply because he has been bidden, without any belief in something outside of himself, then the world just ends. There is no more. All of human history will count for nothing."

His "last act of free will" was my last act of faith. "But I can't do that. I can't take on the responsibility for all mankind. I don't know what to do. If only I had some proof—"

"No proof, Arthur. Proof is the death of faith. That is why I asked you. So again I ask: You know me, but do you believe me?"

I wanted Gabriel's story to be true, to be proof that what I believed was right. But how could I prove myself right, when the mere act of proving it made me wrong?

In the east, the sky was fading to a bleached gray. I could see the trumpet a little better now.

I had to admit, it looked like a very fine instrument.

What's the big deal with Christianity? When we talk about whether "God" exists, why do we always assume we're talking about the Christian concept of God? And how did this once obscure sect get to be the world's largest religion, while the faith upon which it was based now accounts for only 0.02% of the world's population?

During our reading period, we received many time travel stories – typically about going back to the time of the Crucifixion. Those examples of Jesus Christ fan fic were not included in this volume. Ron S. Friedman's work is unique in this way: Rather than going back to King Herod's reign, his intrepid band goes back to that of King Hezekiah – the "savior" of the Judeans whom many Jewish scholars believe the prophet Isaiah was *really* talking about when he wrote, "For unto us a child is born ... Of the increase of his government and peace there shall be no end, upon the throne of David, and upon his kingdom ..."

"BY THE WAY THAT HE CAME"

RON S. FRIEDMAN

When Gideon initiated a routine system check, a red LED flickering on the radar's panel caught his attention.

He adjusted his skullcap and looked carefully through the canopy. The bright, Israeli desert sun forced him to put his hand above his face as he scanned the blue sky.

"Dan," he told the pilot who sat to his left. "You better check this."

"What is it?"

"Looks like a cumulonimbus," he said, referring to a small dark cloud above the horizon.

Captain Dan examined the distant cloud. "Weird. I would have sworn this was a rain cloud if it wasn't August."

As they flew closer, Gideon saw a series of lightning bolts discharged from the cloud. *What in the name of our Lord is it?*

"Eli," shouted the pilot, trying to overcome the helicopter's noise. "Come quick."

Seconds later, Colonel Eli, wearing his olive-drab Tzahal field uniform and carrying his M-16, entered the cockpit.

"What's the excitement about?" asked the colonel.

"Some kind of bizarre storm," replied the pilot, his voice sounded agitated. "We have to plot a new course."

The colonel looked puzzled. "Is that why you called me? I see no reason to change course. Proceed to base as planned."

"Sir, I must protest," said the pilot. "We don't know what that is. It may be dangerous."

"It could be a cluster of hot air for all we know. You have your orders, Captain."

"With all the respect, sir," said Dan, "you know that while the craft is airborne, the sole commander and decision maker is the pilot. And that happens to be me. I say we have to go around this thing."

"Fine," replied the colonel. "Go around. Screw our schedule. You're the boss. But as soon as we land and the craft is no longer airborne, I'll ground you for life."

Gideon felt uncomfortable hearing the two senior officers arguing. Dan was right. Although Eli outranked Dan, infantry officers knew little about flying choppers.

The cloud grew bigger. Gideon swallowed. A spinning cone

formed. It looked like a tornado, except that it rotated horizontally. What in heaven's name is this? From all the storm patterns he had studied during his two-year navigators' course, nothing resembled this phenomenon.

As the Israeli chopper turned north, Gideon followed the mysterious vortex with his eyes. The storm, now to their left, kept growing bigger.

"What's the wind's direction?"

"West," Gideon replied, realizing that the storm was moving in a right angle to the wind.

"It doesn't make any sense," said the pilot.

"Great God!" Gideon shouted as he grabbed his joystick, but there was no need for his intervention since Dan already pulled his all the way.

The massive Sikorsky CH-53 began a sharp turn.

"Hold on tight!" Dan shouted.

A metal cracking sound echoed throughout the chopper. The centrifugal force pushed Gideon to the left. The rotor made screeching noises as the massive helicopter tried to escape the pursuing vortex.

" *Le azazel* ..." Eli shouted in untranslatable Hebrew.

"Hold tight, it's gaining on us!" Dan cried out, cutting the colonel in mid-sentence.

Gideon's eyes widened. The alarm's wail and the flashing red bands of structural damage indicators paralyzed him. Then, all lights died. The whole world turned black.

Quiet.

The wail of the storm was gone. The motor's hum, which Gideon became familiar with, faded away. All that he could hear was the rapid breathing of his comrades, and the spinning blades above.

He felt lightweight. His heart pounded. The chopper started

to lose altitude.

"Turn the engine on! Turn it on!" Dan shouted over the din.

"I can't," cried Gideon, pushing the engine starter button and rolling on the throttle. "No power."

Dan pulled the collective level.

Instinctively, Gideon grabbed the joystick and kicked the pedals, but with a dead engine, his attempt was futile. At least, the spinning rotor slowed down the fall.

"Help us, God," whispered Gideon, thinking of the thirty-three soldiers who flew with them. He took out his pocket Bible and kissed it. "Please."

The helicopter began to spin counter to the main rotor's revolution. Gideon heard wind howling against the chopper's metal body. "*Sh'ma Yisrael, Adonai Eloheynu Adonai Echad.*" He recited, as he saw the ground racing toward them.

Gideon's body brutally absorbed the blow. If he hadn't been restrained in his seat, he would have smashed his head against the instrument panel. Deafening noise roared throughout the chopper's belly. He opened his eyes and looked into the cargo bay. Men and equipment were scattered all around. One soldier shouted in pain. He heard groans, but he couldn't pinpoint the source. Gideon checked for injuries, verifying that he was still in one piece.

Taking a deep breath, Gideon wondered what went wrong. But the most important question that went through his mind was the nature of the mysterious vortex, of which there was suddenly no trace.

A moment passed. The impact dust began to sink. Gideon saw Colonel Eli standing in the mess of twisted people and gear.

"Search for fuel leaks," the colonel commanded his platoon sergeant, "and make sure everyone is okay."

Captain Dan untied himself from the pilot's seat. He walked

through fragments of shattered glass toward the colonel. "Are we on schedule yet?"

Eli's face turned red; he clumped his hand into a fist. "Call base," he said flatly. "Report a crash landing. And Captain," he added, "as you can see, we're not airborne anymore."

"I was about to do that, sir," Dan ground his teeth. He turned his back to the colonel and returned to the shattered cockpit. "Hornet to Hornet Nest, over. Hornet calling Nest, please respond." Gideon heard nothing but static. "I'll try other channels," Dan said.

Eli scratched his head. "Hand me the map, Gideon."

"Yes, sir."

Eli stared at the 100,000-to-1 scale map of central Israel. After a long moment, he gazed at the windows. "We should be halfway between Palmachim and Jerusalem. This area is heavily populated. I wonder why we don't see any lights."

The sergeant returned from his round. "I didn't smell any fuel leaks, sir. And ... I counted seven injured men. Benny is treating them." He said, referring to the platoon's medic. "All minor injuries. No fatalities."

Eli wiped his forehead with his sleeve.

Gideon whispered to Dan. "Did you see that? The Lord is watching over us. Wasn't it the hand of God that allowed us to survive?"

"That God of yours is weird. If he could save our butts, couldn't he made the extra effort and prevent the crash, or better yet, hold back the vortex?"

"How do you know the storm is not an act of God?" asked Gideon. "Who is to say we were not meant to crash here? Don't tell me you believe the vortex was a natural cyclone that just happened to be in our way."

"You depress me, man," said Dan.

Gideon just looked at Captain Dan, and coughed.

"Are you feeling all right?"

"I'm fine, thanks."

"I hope it's not the swine flu." Dan chuckled.

"Very funny."

"Sir," Dan turned his head toward the Colonel, "No luck on the radio. I tried various channels, no reply. GPS is not working either. I even tried other frequencies, FM, AM – nothing. No radio communication whatsoever."

Eli settled on a broken box under the emergency light. He released a deep breath. "I want to know where we are and what is going on," he said, staring at the sergeant. "In one hour."

"Yes, sir."

The colonel stood up facing his platoon. "The rest of you ladies, pack your gear. We're moving out."

"Sir?" Benny asked.

"What is it, Private?"

"I was trying to call home from my cell. All I'm getting is 'Network not found.'"

"Thank you, sweetie, I hope you don't miss your mommy. Now move your behind and help the wounded out of here. On the double."

Many of the soldiers laughed.

Even though these troops were on a trial period for Sayeret Tzanhanim – the paratroopers reconnaissance unit – and the colonel was expected to treat them as if he was a drill sergeant, Gideon felt sorry for Benny. The memories of his own flying course trial period were still fresh.

The platoon set up a defensive perimeter around the helicopter. Captain Dan remained at the cockpit. The night was unusually quiet. No sounds of passing cars, trucks, or commercial airlines. No noise except for some jackal howling or the occasional knocking sound from the cockpit, which Gideon imagined was Captain Dan banging his head against the wall.

An hour later, a clear voice came out of the tactical radio. "Screwdriver calling Hornet."

Eli jumped as if he was bitten by a snake. Everyone's eyes turned to the radio. It was the sergeant's voice.

"Go on, Screwdriver."

"I have a visual on an isolated farm, about ten clicks to the south, and on some campfires about twelve clicks to the south west."

"Continue."

"And ... and ... no visual on Highway One." Everyone knew the designation of the main road from Tel Aviv to Jerusalem.

Eli stared at the map. Then he glanced at his watch. He took a handkerchief and wiped his forehead. "That's impossible." He brought the mic to his mouth and clicked on the button. "Return to Hornet."

"Got it."

Except for the first watch, the platoon retired for the night. Gideon covered himself with an army issued sleeping bag. He coughed once more. I think I'm developing a flu.

At first light, someone shook Gideon's shoulder. He opened his eyes and saw Colonel Eli standing above him.

"Rise and shine."

"Why, what?"

"We're going on patrol, and you're coming with me."

Gideon coughed. "Sorry." He straightened up, feeling a horrible headache. "Why do you need me for? I'm just an aircrewman."

"Did you do basic training?"

"Of course."

"Then get your weapon and mov ..." Eli stopped, as if realizing Gideon was a fellow officer and not one of his pawns. "You're a navigator." He changed his tone. "I need your help to find out where we are."

Gideon would have preferred to be called a systems operator, or a copilot. However, the traditional name 'navigator' seemed to stick as his job title.

He nodded, and joined a small detachment of troops. He prayed he could make it through the day without calling in sick.

The squad set course south, toward the farm. The rest of the platoon remained behind to assist the pilot repairing the chopper.

After a one-hour forced march, the squad reached a ridge overlooking the farm. Colonel Eli made a gesture with his right hand. The men immediately lay down.

Gideon felt his blood rushing as he crawled uphill. It was like basic training, but for real.

From the top, he saw three people standing near a hut surrounded by olive trees. Gideon raised his binoculars. The larger view revealed seven horses tied to the trees. The people wore brown leather armor. They carried large swords and short bows, their heads covered by black pointy helmets. They spoke among themselves in a language Gideon couldn't understand.

Suddenly, the door flew open. Gideon heard shouting. Three more armored men pushed out a ragged old man and young woman with long braided hair. The six circled the man and the woman and started kicking them, laughing as they did.

Benny stood up.

"What are you doing, soldier?" Colonel Eli whispered. "The locals are not our concern."

Gideon held his breath. Down by the hut, one of the men drew a sword from a scabbard at his hip, and stabbed the old man. The other laughed and yelled something incomprehensible.

The woman screamed in terror and cried, "Father!" Then she faced the armored men, "You killed him. Bastards!"

"Hey, she's speaking Hebrew," Gideon said.

Her accent was strange, the pronunciation awkward, yet Gideon could clearly understand her.

"You're right," Eli said, then paused for a moment to ponder the situation. "You two," he told the soldiers who carried the Negev machine gun, "stay here and cover our backs." Then he turned to the other soldiers, "We'll take them peacefully. If they become hostile, drop them!"

"Yes sir," replied the men.

The group of soldiers charged downhill brandishing their rifles. The six men left the woman alone, and turned to face the soldiers, drawing their swords. Even though they were outnumbered and outgunned, they seemed unafraid and ready for combat. The two groups of men came face-to-face ten yards apart and stood still. The leader of the six shouted something out. Gideon thought he recognized the language. Quietly, he repeated the leader's words. Then he whispered, "This cannot be ..."

"We're Tzahal. Drop your weapons!" Eli commanded, bringing the butt of his rifle to his shoulder. "Lie face down on the ground, while you still have a face. I'm going to count to one."

The young woman, shouted, "Look out!"

An arrow streaked through the air, striking Benny in the chest. Simultaneously, the sword-wielding men charged at the soldiers, blades raised above their heads. The soldiers opened fire. Five of the swordsmen were immediately gunned down before they could even land a single blow, but the sixth got in range and swung his sword at Gideon's head. Gideon parried with his rifle. They clashed and rolled on the ground, grappling with each other. *BANG!* A shot was heard, and the swordsman stopped moving. Gideon looked up, above him stood Eli, smoke dissolving from his M-16.

"Thanks," said Gideon.

"There!" The woman shouted pointing at the hut. An archer wearing leather armor stood in the doorway, pulling his bowstring for another shot. *BANG!* Eli's shot hit the archer's arm, and he dropped the bow.

Benny lay on the ground with an arrow sticking out of his chest. Gideon watched Eli walking to check his condition. "I'm fine." Benny said.

He sat up and pulled off his bulletproof ceramic vest and examined the arrow.

"Not injured, eh?" said Eli. "That's nice of you to lie down while the rest of us are doing all the fighting." He smiled and helped Benny stand. "Being a medic, would you be kind enough to check the old man?"

The woman knelt, cradling her father's head, sobbing. Benny bent beside her and checked the old man's pulse. He looked at Eli, and shook his head.

Two soldiers tied the captive archer, who shouted and tried to break free, but was easily restrained.

Gideon listened to the prisoner's words. Good Lord. Could it be? No, it can't be. But then again … He approached the colonel, "Sir, I think I recognize that language."

Eli raised his eyebrows.

"It's Aramaic."

"Aramaic?" Eli repeated the word, as if refusing to believe. "I thought that language had been dead for two thousand years." He looked into Gideon's eyes. "You know Aramaic?"

"I learned it as part of my Talmud studies."

"Interesting," Eli said, shaking his head. "And how would he know Aramaic?" He pointed his finger at the archer. "Somehow, these guys don't strike me as the types who study in a yeshiva."

Gideon shrugged.

Eli turned his head to the wounded archer. "Can you speak with him?"

Gideon looked at the archer. He wasn't fluent in Aramaic. He knew how to read the Talmud. He knew the Passover songs. He'd never tried to conduct a conversation in Aramaic with another person, though.

"I told the prisoner that we're Israeli soldiers." Gideon briefed Eli after the interrogation. "He didn't believe me. He claimed that Israel was destroyed twenty years ago. He also said, and that's really weird, that he is an Assyrian."

Eli took off his helmet and scratched the back of his head. "Twenty years ago? That's ridiculous. When I was a kid, some freaks used to say the world would come to an end, but I clearly remember that it didn't."

Eli turned to Benny, who was treating the woman. "How is she?"

"Passed out. She took quite a beating."

Dear God. Gideon gripped his head with both hands. Almost a century and a half before the Babylonians sacked Solomon's temple, the Assyrians destroyed the northern kingdom of Israel and expelled the ten so-called 'lost' tribes; the lost tribes. He wished he had learned more Bible instead of focusing on Talmud. He pulled out his book, and started browsing through it.

It took him a few minutes to find what he was looking for.

"Look sir, at the Bible, 18:13, the Second Book of Kings."

"Gideon, we don't have time for this. Try to extract more intel from the hostile."

"Sir, just listen to this."

Without waiting for approval, Gideon read aloud, "'And in the fourteenth year of King Hezekiah did Sennacherib the King of Assyria come up against all the fortified cities of Judea and took them …'"

"What is this crap?" Eli raised his eyebrows. "Are you saying that these guys think that they belong to the army of Senach-ch-ch-ch … – whatever that king's name is? Is there a madhouse nearby?"

"Do you know any madhouse that teaches Aramaic?"

"Then what's your explanation?" Eli looked straight at Gideon's eyes.

"I think God sent us, um, to the time of King Hezekiah." Gideon began to reflect the meaning of these words. All the pieces were starting to pull together, the awe-inspiring vortex, the lack of radio communication, GPS or Highway One; no lights or passing airplanes. "Oh, my God!"

The archer was dragged out of the hut. Benny and another soldier created a makeshift stretcher for the woman. The rests were getting ready to move out. A small burial mound in the sand marked the old man's final resting place.

"In your Bible …" Eli asked Gideon, "the Assyrian army – how big is it?"

"A hundred fourscore and five thousand."

"How many?"

Gideon coughed, "One hundred and eighty five thousand, marching on Jerusalem."

There was an awkward moment of silence, eventually broken by Dan's voice, "Screwdriver from Hornet. The bird is ready, what's your location?"

Eli took the mic. "We are on Foxtrot, ten clicks from Hornet. We're on our way home."

Glancing at his watch, Eli shouted at his troops. "Time to dress up, ladies. We don't want to be late for the ball."

The soldiers picked up their gear and paced into the Judean hills, carrying the wounded Assyrian and the woman on two stretchers.

Gideon approached the woman. She wore crude clothing. Although she was smelly, beneath the filth, she didn't look bad, not bad at all ...

Gideon wiped her pale face with a wet cloth. She opened her eyes and looked at him. Her pupils widened.

"Do not fear. We're Israeli soldiers. My name is Gideon."

"I'm Miriam, daughter of Nathan. My father, where is he?"

"He is with God now. There was nothing we could do but lay him to his final rest. I'm sorry."

"Where are you taking me?"

"To our helico ... You will be safer with us."

Miriam laid her head on the stretcher and passed out.

Gideon was amazed how he, a modern Israeli, could speak with a woman using Biblical Hebrew. He thanked God for all those years of studying ancient text and old prayers.

By late afternoon, the dust-covered squad returned to the crash landing site. The soldiers in the camp followed the prisoner and the ragged woman with their eyes. Gideon shivered; he felt was about to collapse. "If it wasn't for the flu," he sighed.

"Dan and Gideon – briefing," barked the colonel.

Gideon's only desire was to crawl back into his sleeping bag.

"I can't explain what happened last night," said Eli after they sat down, "but somehow we were pulled back in time." Eli's eyes were fixed on the pilot. "Captain Dan, the intelligence we recovered from our 'guests' confirms we're now in the year 701 B.C.E."

There was a brief moment of silence. The pilot's eyes narrowed. He burst into laughter. "You're kidding, right?" Then he stood up and started to walk toward the chopper. "I almost believed you were serious. I'll try calling base again."

"Sit down, Dan!"

"It's true," Gideon said. "The Lord of Hosts brought us here."

Dan froze; he looked straight at Gideon, his skullcap and his Bible. "You're not joking."

Eli shook his head. "And we need to decide what to do next."

"Time travel?" Dan released a deep breath. "Impossible! Though that might explain the radio silence and the lack of any modern landmarks."

Gideon and Eli shrugged.

"Assuming you're right," said Dan, "and I ain't saying that you are, will it be possible to go back? I mean, forward in time to where … when we come from?"

"I don't really know," answered Eli flatly, his fingers tipped on his M-16's butt.

"What I know," added Gideon, "is that we're not going back before fulfilling the Lord's plan for us."

"701 B.C.E.?" Dan asked. "Which part of the world?"

"According to the topography – Judea. Not far from Lachish," Gideon said.

"Hmm," mumbled Dan. "King Solomon died sometime around 930 B.C.E., then the kingdom was split in half. Israel in the north and Judea in the south. The Northern Kingdom was destroyed two hundred years later by the Assyrians. Judea remained independent until occupied by Babylon. Anything significant happened in 701 B.C.E.?"

"Yes," Eli said.

The colonel pointed his fingers at the surrounding hills, "701 was the year Assyria invaded Judea. Assyria is the regional superpower. According to our yeshiva boy, Gideon, the invading force is 185,000 strong."

At first, Dan said nothing. He stared at the colonel with his eyes wide open. "185,000? Bullshit. Alexander the Great only had 40,000 troops."

"But the Bible clearly said 185,000." Dan's disbelief seemed unreasonable to Gideon. "Do you doubt it?"

"The prisoner we interrogated was a member of a small raiding force," Eli told Dan. "Most of the Assyrian army is now preparing to besiege Jerusalem."

"This is madness." Dan shook his head and then he massaged his temples. "Total madness."

"This is God's will," replied Gideon. "God sent us here for a purpose."

"We must release the prisoner and remain neutral." Dan said flatly. "Let's not do anything that might jeopardize our historical timeline."

Eli shook his head, "We have a chance to change history for the better. We can bring electricity, antibiotics, democracy and …"

"Are you out of your mind?" snapped Dan. "We can do irreversible damage to our history without even knowing it. Look at Gideon, he appears sick."

Gideon nodded, "It's nothing serious, sir. Only a flu."

"Only a flu? Only a flu you say? That's a perfect example of how deadly something that appears harmless can be. Do you remember the panic around the swine flu and the bird flu? Do you know why flu was so feared? I'll tell you why. Because it was a new strain. One unrecognized by our immune system. Now imagine introducing a modern set of flu strains, diseases that our immune system had three thousand years to cope with!"

"What's your point?" asked Gideon.

"Did you know that during the years 1918 to 1919 more than twenty million people died of influenza? Did you know that diseases brought from Europe by the first Spanish conquistadors killed 95 percent of the American natives in fewer than sixty years? Most of them from harmless European chickenpox."

"None of that matters," Gideon felt he was about to explode. "God sent the vortex. The Lord transferred us back in time to save Jerusalem." He took out the small pocket Bible he carried. "The vortex was no a random event. Our mission is to help King Hezekiah." He opened the book. "Here, look ..."

"Are you nuts?" Dan snapped. "Kings in Jerusalem? Hello! Eli, we are soldiers of a twenty-first century democratic country. We can't make decisions based on suggestions of this fundamentalist fanatic," he said pointing at Gideon.

"If God didn't send us here," Gideon tried to remain calm, "perhaps you have an alternative explanation as to the natural or artificial phenomenon that transferred us 2,700 years into the past?"

For a long moment, Dan said nothing. "I can't," eventually he whispered. "But even though it's unexplainable, that doesn't mean divine intervention."

"What will it take to convince you?" asked Gideon. "Are you expecting God to appear before you like he did before Moses on Mount Sinai?"

Dan shrugged. "That would definitely help."

"Perhaps," replied Gideon, "but unnecessary. Once we complete our quest, it will become apparent even to you that we were brought here for a single purpose."

"Okay, you win. I give up." Dan raised his hands. "Assuming God wants us to help this King Hezekiah. What can we do? We are only one platoon. Each of us carries five hundred bullets. We have four thousand rounds for the Vulcan and a few grenades. Even if we kill one Assyrian with every shot, which is impossible even under the best circumstances, we will still be facing 165,000 of the alleged 185,000. Frankly, we can't save Jerusalem, even if we want to."

"Hmm," said Eli. "Pizarro conquered the Inca Empire with fewer than two hundred people, and without automatic weapons. If two thousand Assyrians could be blown to pieces in one short barrage, it would destroy their morale and scatter their army."

Gideon raised his book, "But the Bible clearly says ..."

"Gideon, not now..." snapped Eli.

"Excuse me, sir." The debate between the officers was interrupted by Benny. "Miriam is sick. She wants to see Gideon."

"How are you doing, Miriam?"

She sat on her stretcher, her face pale. A few blood smears suggested her nose was bleeding. When she saw Gideon, she tried to smile, but only coughed.

"You look troubled, Gideon. What is it?"

"I think I know what the future holds, but not how to get there."

"No one but the great prophets at the gates of Jerusalem knows what the future holds."

"And the Lord Almighty."

"Did God send you to save us from the Assyrians?"

"It appears so."

"Where did you come from?" she asked.

"I was born in Jerusalem."

"I was in Jerusalem once. My father and I took a pilgrimage to the Temple of Solomon when I was ten years old. I shall never forget how beautiful it was. As we went up the road to the Temple Mount, I could feel myself being shrouded by the holiness of this place. And the temple itself ... all covered in gold and gemstones. And then the high priest came out, all dressed in white – just as I imagined an Angel of the Lord to look like."

"I wish I could see that."

"Gideon, I'm sick."

"I know. Don't worry Miriam. You'll be fine. Benny has antibio ... hmm, Benny can cure you."

"They're coming!" The sentry on duty shouted. "They're coming! Huge force!"

Outside the medical tent, Gideon heard Eli issuing orders, "We're moving out. Dan, start the motors. Now!"

Soldiers jumped out of their sleeping bags and ran toward the gray bird. Some came to help Benny with the wounded. Others helped the pilot with the engines. Gideon carried Miriam into the cargo bay. A crunch was heard as Dan tried to start the giant motor.

Distant sounds of trumpets and drums rippled throughout the camp. The motor made some snoring noises, refusing to ignite.

The first Assyrian battalion became visible on top of the nearby ridge. A few hundred spearmen, shield carriers, and archers, accompanied by five or six chariots waved their weapons while shouting something incomprehensible. They gave the impression they were about to attack the isolated platoon.

"We don't have enough juice in the battery," shouted Dan. "Shove the blades."

Six soldiers threw ropes and captured the top of the propeller. They started to pull. Slowly, the rotor began to spin. The engine coughed, then ignited. The big vessel rumbled as the blades picked up speed.

"Everybody in, *yalla, yalla!* Are you waiting for a special invitation?"

"We'll safe inside this ... this flying carriage," Gideon told Miriam.

"Flying carriage? Like Elijah?"

Gideon nodded.

A burst of gunshots ended their conversation. Gideon looked for the source. The Assyrian archer lied on the ground holding his leg, crying in pain.

The sentry shrugged, "He tried to escape, so I fired a warning shot. He didn't stop. What was I supposed to do?"

"What was that noise?" Miriam asked Gideon. "Is a thunderstorm breaking?"

Gideon looked at her, amazed at the difference in perspectives between him and the people of that time. "Yes, sort of. We have lots of those where I come from."

"Like an Angel of the Lord."

Gideon held her hand, "I must leave you now with Benny. I must help navigate this flying carriage."

The Assyrian battalion stopped when they heard the mighty dreadnought roar. As it took off, they took a few steps back. The war bird hovered above the hillside. From his seat beside the pilot, Gideon could see their old camp swarmed by hundreds of plunder-thirsty Assyrians.

"We have about five hours of fuel," said Dan. "Where would you like to go, sir?"

"Up!" Eli shouted over the rotors' noise. "Do you want to stay here and politely ask the Assyrian army for directions?"

Eli wiped the sweat off his forehead. "The State of Israel doesn't exist yet and the Israeli army won't be here for another 2700 years," the colonel sighed. "As unbelievable as it may sound, we're legally bound to serve Israel's predecessor, the Kingdom of Judea. We are going to offer our services to King Hezekiah. Set course to Jerusalem."

"Sir," Dan said, "I must advise against it. Gideon, tell him. Does it say anywhere in your holy book about a helicopter landing in Jerusalem?"

Gideon didn't reply.

Under the moonlight, about ten miles to the east, Gideon saw the walls and the tower tops of ancient Jerusalem. The wind blew in through the Sikorsky's broken windows. He shivered when his gaze fell upon the dark, sluggish, never-ending mass of Assyrians slowly circling the holy city.

Silence prevailed in the chopper. It was a full moon, the sun was about to rise. The dimming figure of the City of David and glimmer of Solomon's Temple filled Gideon's heart with awe.

The war bird hovered above Zion, its projector illuminating the streets. Under the search light, Gideon saw people pouring into the alleys, cheering and dancing. Tears flooded his eyes. "I can't see any suitable landing zone."

"Is this what I think it is?" Dan said.

Gideon looked through the broken window; he wiped his eyes in disbelief.

"Eli," shouted Dan, "a vortex is forming to our west. Maybe we can go back to the future."

Gideon felt the high g-force as the giant bird made a sharp turn.

"We can't go home, yet," cried Gideon. "We haven't completed God's mission."

"Perhaps God doesn't want us to save Jerusalem. Have you

considered that?" Dan shouted, overcoming the engine's racket.

"Colonel?" screamed Gideon.

"Turn this bird back to Jerusalem," shouted Eli. "Do you copy?"

"Sir," replied Dan, "with all due respect, you keep forgetting, sir, that when we're airborne, your ass is mine."

"Do you realize how many Assyrians we see here?" Gideon looked at Dan. "If we don't help, Jerusalem will fall. Millions will die. The fate of the Jewish people will be identical to the fate of the ten lost tribes. Look!" He pointed his index finger at the massive army below. "If we do nothing, there will be no Judea, no Jews, no Jesus, Christianity or Islam. This is why God sent us here."

Dan stared at the vortex. "You didn't answer my question, Gideon. Why did God send us this vortex prematurely? Why is God showing us a way to return home if he wants us to fight the Assyrians?"

"Choice." replied Gideon. "It's always about making a choice. God gave a choice to Job, to Abraham, to Lot and to Adam."

"Then I choose home," said Dan.

"What home?" Gideon tried to appeal to Dan's logic. "If the Assyrian army remains intact, Assyria will be invincible. It will crush the Babylonian rebellion. That means no Babylonian Empire, which will profoundly impact on the Persian Empire, the Greeks, and the Romans."

"Gideon, you can't change history. The Assyrians won't win because they didn't win in the past. Our duty is to our passengers and their families. We're going home."

Gideon thought about taking the joystick and diverting the course back to Jerusalem. But Dan would fight him. The troops who wanted to go home, would support Dan. Gideon looked at the approaching cyclone. There was only one thing he could do.

And although it seemed impossible, he still had his faith in God.

"I'm sorry, Dan," Gideon said, as he untied himself. "I have to go."

Gideon knelt beside Miriam, holding her hand. He wished he could have said goodbye, explain what he was about to do. But he couldn't. "Take this. Read it." He gave her his Bible.

"I can't read."

"Please, for me."

She took it. Tears appeared in her eyes.

Gideon stood up. He scanned the floor. One of the soldiers left his battle vest and weapon unsecured. He grabbed them and put them on. It felt heavy with all the extra magazines and hand grenades.

"What are you doing?" cried Benny.

Gideon pulled the emergency door handle. The external wicket lid was immediately sucked by the vortex. Flashes of lightning illuminated the chopper's interior. Sheets of rain lashed at Gideon's face.

"Gideon, answer me. What are you doing?" Benny untied himself and jumped at Gideon.

"Let me go, Benny."

"No! You can't do that!" Benny grasped Gideon and lifted him off the floor. They both fell and rolled over each other. "Help me!" Benny cried toward the soldiers, "Stop this maniac! He wants to jump!"

With his elbow, Gideon landed a Krav Maga blow into Benny's face. "I know what I'm doing," he shouted. "It's all written down in the Scripture."

A few soldiers came to Benny's aid. Still on his back, Gideon kneed Benny in the ribs. Benny flinched and let go. Two other soldiers tried to seize Gideon's leg. It was too late. Gideon dived out.

Standing before the Assyrian commander, Gideon spat blood on the ground. His hands were tied, and his M-16 had been taken away from him. He didn't care much about it since he had already run out of bullets.

"You thought you could kill the entire Assyrian army with your thunder staff?" The commander raised his finger, and another lash hit Gideon's back. "Pathetic."

"God will have his revenge." Gideon coughed again. "Jerusalem will be spared." He spoke Aramaic.

The commander burst into a rolling laughter. "Fool. Nothing will save Zion. In a few days, King Hezekiah will be in chains, his queen and daughters will be mine. I'll let the soldiers play with them before I sell them in Nineveh's slave market."

Gideon coughed.

"Your friends ran like scared sheep when our battalions arrived at the place where the big metal bird rested."

Gideon coughed.

"Your feeble god can't even save you. How can he save Jerusalem?" This time, the Assyrian commander coughed.

"It was never God's intention to spare my life." Gideon raised his bleeding head. "I don't suppose you ever heard of influenza?"

Below, Eli saw lights. These were car lights, traveling on the oh-so-familiar Highway One.

"How can it be?" He looked once more at the modern traffic below.

"Angels," Miriam said. "He was an angel of the Lord." She extended her hand. She held something. A small book.

Eli took the Bible and started to read from the marked location. "Dan, you better hear this," he said.

"'And it came to pass that night, that the angel of Jehovah went forth, and smote in the camp of the Assyrians a hundred fourscore and five thousand: and when men arose early in the morning, behold, these were all dead bodies.'"

The Second Book of Kings, 19:35

ABOUT THE CONTRIBUTORS

Jennifer Rachel Baumer lives, writes and runs in the Northern Nevada desert. Her work has appeared in Nevada's *Danse Macabre* magazine, in *Lady Churchill's Rosebud Wristlet*, in Sky Warrior Books' *Healing Waves* charity anthology, and in a variety of genre anthologies and magazines. She's ghostwritten 14 nonfiction books for experts, and is marketing her own novels. Jennifer shares her desert life with her husband Rick and an abnormal number of cats, both indoor types and the bobcats that pass through her yard.

Brandon H. Bell is a writer of weird fiction and co-editor of *The AetherAge: Helios* anthology and *Fantastique Unfettered* magazine. His work has appeared in publications from *Hadley Rille* and *M-Brane SF*, as well as venues such as *The Lovecraft eZine*, *Everyday Weirdness*, and *Eschatology Journal*. He is a member of the Outer Alliance (supporting his GBLTQ counterparts in the genre community) and a Rissho Kosei-kai Buddhist. He is working on a novel about alien megalodons, Dali elephants, and a patchwork of human religions in the Alpha Centauri system. He can be found online at nithska.blogspot.com or via Google profile +Brandon H. Bell.

Patrick Evans is a Toronto writer who has published short fiction in the *James White Review, Contra/Diction: New Queer Male Fiction*, and the *Fresh Blood* anthology for writers who are new to the horror genre. As a journalist he worked for the *Toronto Star* where he won the Canadian Association of

Journalists Award for Investigative Journalism and covered everything from gangland slayings to shopping for a convincing toupee.

David J. Fielding is an actor and writer currently residing in the city of Pittsburgh. He has a BFA and a MFA, both in acting. Throughout his career he has worked in film, TV, radio, the stage and provided voice overs for video games. David is probably best known as the face and voice of Zordon from the *Mighty Morphin' Power Rangers*. David provided the voice for the first season, though his image continued to be the face of Zordon for many seasons. In addition to his stage and film work, David has provided voice work for a number of popular PC video games, including *Empire Earth* and *Dungeon Siege: Legends of Aranna*. He is currently finishing up a novel and several other short works of fiction.

William Freedman is a satirist who uses science fiction and fantasy tropes. He is author of *Land That I Love* and the soon-to-be-released *Mighty Mighty*, co-author with Ben Parris of *Supernaturalz*, contributor to the 2005 *Spirit House* chapbook to raise money for tsunami survivors, and a frequent program participant at genre conventions throughout the northeast U.S. His non-fiction bylines – covering everything from hot stocks for *Investor's Business Daily* to the rise of distilled spirits for *History* magazine to Bram Stoker Awards weekend for Long Island's *Newsday* – go back more than 20 years.

Ron S. Friedman has seen his short stories appear in *Daily Science Fiction*, and received an Honorable Mention in the Writers of the Future contest. He is on the Canadian Science Fiction and Fantasy Association board of directors, a When Worlds Collide festival member-at-large and a member of the Imaginative Fiction Writers Association. He has appeared as a panelist at a number of genre conventions. Ron is currently working on his second novel. His *Age of Certainty* story was partially inspired by Ron's experiences during his service in the Israeli Air Force in the late 1980s and early 1990s.

James Hartley is a former computer programmer. Originally from northern New Jersey, he now lives in sunny central Florida. He has published six fantasy novels, *The Ghost of Grover's Ridge, Magic Is Faster Than Light, Teen Angel, Cop with a Wand, Magic to the Rescue* and *This Wand for Hire*, and has one more, *Fortunatus*, due out soon. He has had short stories published as e-books, in the collections *Five from the Future, Five from the Faerie*, and *Worlds Away and Worlds Aweird*, in anthologies, and in various e-zines and print magazines. He is currently working on a new novel, *Magic versus the Empire*. He is a member of IWOFA and the Dark Fiction Guild. His website is ***http://teenangel.netfirms.com***.

Brian K. Lowe works as a legal assistant in Los Angeles by day, and writes at night in a candlelit garret with only a small fire to ward off the chill of the frigid Southern California nights. His work has appeared in *Daily Science Fiction, Buzzy Mag, White Cat* and a number of other publications. You can learn more at his blog at ***brianklowe@wordpress.com***.

James Morrow has been writing fiction ever since, at age seven, he dictated "The Story of the Dog Family" to his mother, who dutifully typed it up and bound the pages with yarn. Upon reaching adulthood, Morrow wrote such satiric novels as *Towing Jehovah* (World Fantasy Award), *Blameless in Abaddon* (a New York Times Notable Book of the Year), *The Last Witchfinder* (called "an inventive feat" by critic Janet Maslin), and *The Philosopher's Apprentice* ("an ingenious riff on Frankenstein" according to NPR). His short fiction has won the

Nebula Award (twice), the Rickie Award, and the Theodore Sturgeon Memorial Award.

Élena Nazzaro is an illustrator and watercolorist. Her work has been featured in *Artist's Sketchbook* magazine, *Kiwi*, *Building Letters*, and regular feature with illustrated full-color spreads in *Craft: Magazine's* "The Art of Cooking." She has collaborated in the past with editor Bill Freedman on *Spirit House* and illustrated the short story collection *Spirits Unwrapped*. By day she is the art director at PRI. She can be found online at frenchtoastgirl.com.

Ian R. Thorpe's earliest ambition, after he gave up on being a train driver, was to write. Life plays strange tricks and, despite some early successes including his work being performed on national radio and television and minor prizes for poetry and short fiction, he pursued a lucrative career in information technology. This pushed other interests aside for many years and only when illness forced a change of lifestyle did he start writing again. Ian lives in Lancashire, U.K.

Jeffrey Witthauer has seen his work appear in Paradigm Concepts' *Arcanis* and *Witch Hunter: The Invisible World* series of tabletop roleplaying games, the latter of which takes place in an alternate seventeenth century where there is divine certainty.

www.ingramcontent.com/pod-product-compliance
Lightning Source LLC
Chambersburg PA
CBHW030334180626
46810CB00003B/1359